Brothas from
Anotha Motha

BROTHAS FROM ANOTHA MOTHA

Timothy "TBone" Hicks

authorHOUSE®

AuthorHouse™ LLC
1663 Liberty Drive
Bloomington, IN 47403
www.authorhouse.com
Phone: 1-800-839-8640

Published by AuthorHouse 07/28/2014

ISBN: 978-1-4969-2968-6 (sc)
ISBN: 978-1-4969-2955-6 (e)

CHAPTER 1

"A mind is a terrible thing to waste."

BOC! The .45-caliber baby missile rocketed through Parnell's cerebral cortex, passing through his membrane and exiting through his frontal lobe. Brain fragments and blood splattered all over the inside of the front windshield. A gaping hole buzzed out all the thoughts, hopes, and dreams of young Parnell as formaldehyde blew through the hole in the windshield that the bullet left. Young Parnell's head slumped to the side and came to rest on the passenger side door panel of Rick's old-school Cutlass.

"Damn, Jason, blood, why you couldn't wait 'til we got to the hills, man?" Rick yelled, startled and pissed off. "You dun fucked up my old school with this snitch-ass nigga's brains and shit all over it!"

"Fuck this car, nigga!" Jason said. "I got tired of hearing that nigga's mouth. Bitch-ass nigga wouldn't shut the fuck up, so I dun it for 'em! That's what's wrong with these new booty-ass niggas nowadays, they just don't know when to shut the fuck up! I try to tell them little niggas a brain is a terrible thing to waste all the time, shit!"

"Well, nigga, you diggin' da ditch, and you cleaning out my car too," spat Rick.

"I don't give a fuck, nigga. It ain't the first mutha-fuckin' ditch I dun dug, nigga. Just drive this bitch up there," Jason shot out.

Rick maneuvered the Cutty through the dark eve of the murderous streets of Oakland, California. Rick and Jason were probably responsible for over one-third of the city's rising crime rate this year. The crime rate was already 114 and only half the year was gone. Jason and Rick, or Rick and Jason I should say, grew inseparable. The only fight or dispute they'd ever had, and still have to this day, is whose name is said first when people talk about them. They both came from the projects, living in dilapidated Cambel Village only a few doors down from one another. Oakland has a lot of rundown, poverty-stricken, dope-fiend-infested, vacant buildings; crack-controlled, heroin-syringed, littered, over-polluted, weed-baggy spots in it. But West Oakland is a little bit grimmer than the east and the north sides of the town; just a little.

Thirteen years earlier

Rick was born only two days before Jason, so he always felt that he was the oldest. The pair had two life-changing experiences on the same exact day. Rick walked his junior high school sweetheart, Erica, home from school one day. After kissing her luscious lips and palming her pretty brown round, he left her for home, sporting an aura of love that only Valentine's Day can bring. He was an only child and his momma made sure he always had the best and that he didn't want for nothing. She worked two jobs to ensure her baby would not need to resort to the streets and be lost like the daddy he never knew. His light skin was rash with heat from the sun. His green eyes squinted for focus as he wiped the sweat off his newly cut fade. His hair was brown, but since his dad was white, he had what they might call "good hair."

Rick's Nike Cortez tennis shoes hit the ground in stride as he turned the corner on Chestnut. When he saw all those red and blue lights illuminating on top of black-and-white police cars, his gut felt queasy. Something in his heart told him that something was wrong with his momma. He picked up stride and burst into the crowd of onlookers and spectators. Yellow tape surrounded his building as police officers controlled the crowd. He saw Jason sitting off to the side with floods of tears streaming down his cheeks.

Jason always cut school and never gave a fuck about his dope-fiend momma. His dad, his cool-ass dad, never complained about taking care of his only son. His dad's only regret was the vessel he chose to carry his seed in. But back in the day, Charlene was most likely to succeed, and most attractive in the high school yearbook. They were even crowned King and Queen of the "Best Couples." But Jason Darren

Hill Sr. became a single father and a lonely king of his project castle when Charlene ran out, chasing the crack monster. Jason Sr. always found himself saving Charlene's life from all the young dealers who would demand their dough from him. Although she stopped physically living with her family, Charlene was always making frequent appearances when she paraded the neighborhood on her crack binge. Jason Jr., like his dad, watched her out of the dark, pain-filled brown eyes of his as she tricked with local prospects. Jason Sr. worked a regular job and provided every need for his son physically, while his mother provided his emotional needs.

After realizing that he was no match for the police barricade and being shuffled off, Rick made his way through an open gap and to his best friend, Jason.

"Jay, what's wrong, man? What happened?" Rick asked, consumed with worry.

Jason's dark skin reeked of blood, sweat, and tears. Even his "TWA" (teeny-weeny afro) was drenched. He had the blackest little hands and those kind of nails that are naturally black and bitten down to the nubs. He looked up at Rick and pointed sadly to the police car. Rick's eyes followed Jason's finger and tear-filled eyes to the back seat of the police cruiser, where Charlene sat. She sat calmly, but she perspired heavily, and her wig sat crooked on the top of her crack-filled black head. She looked and smiled the smile of victory. Rick didn't understand what her smile meant until Jay told him the whole story.

In a nutshell, Jason's momma killed Jason's dad and Rick's momma because she finally caught them fuckin' after all these years. Her crack courage gave her the strength to confront Jason Sr. and Cathalene McMillan on Valentine's Day. She had been getting high all day and sobbing in her misery of memories. She took one last pull and decided to kill all her memories and them two at the same time. And with it being her and Jason Sr.'s 15th anniversary, that helped her plunge the knife 15 more times into each one of them. Real brutal, and a serious tragedy.

Rick and Jason were separated and forced to live with foster parents for a year and ended up finding one another in East Oakland, grinding on the same block. The bond they had in the past grew stronger when a bullet from each of their guns landed in the chest of a hood rival. Plus, 20 bricks to split made it easy too. Although it was Jason's mom who killed Rick's mom, the love Jason's dad had for Rick's mom overrode Jay's momma's delirious actions. Jason's mom's life sentence helped too. Since they only had each other, they decided that no one or nothing would ever come between them. They even took blood vows. They ran trains on the same hood rats, shared the same apartment, and stacked their dough together. Since the fall of the man of the hood, they became the neighborhood kingpins. They commanded a crew of young hyphy and wild teenagers who only listened to Jay and Rick. Rick was more of the brains and Jay loved blood. Neither one used drugs or got drunk. Jay always felt that being intoxicated made you weak. He figured that would make a person go crazy or make a bad decision. His favorite commercial is the one where the egg fries in the skillet and it states, "This is your brain on drugs." Rick, on the other hand, just simply didn't like to have his chiseled 5'10" frame that he worked out to maintain worn down. Both guys were health-conscious. But Rick took it to the extreme. They tried to stress the rules and importance of not getting high to their crew, but the youngsters never listened to them.

The present

Young Parnell still had his blunt clutched tightly in his fingers when they deposited his body in the bank of the Oakland hills. There was too much DNA in the car, so Rick had to use his better judgment and toast it.

As Rick and Jason sat in their living room on the large, soft, black leather couch, orange juice rested on the glass coffee table right by Jason's feet. Rick picked the carton up and took a swig as their eyes bulged at the 60-inch screen TV. Rick's bare ass was moving in quick rotation as his dick jammed in and out a big black ass. Beads of sweat ran down his face as he pounded away. On the other end of the chocolate specimen, Jason's black hand held the back of her head while his dick appeared, then disappeared in her mouth. She handled both ends like a seasoned vet. Both Jay and Rick slapped five and looked at the camera and gave a cheesecake grin and pointed. Off the screen they look at each other and slapped five again to celebrate another hood rat taken down to the block monsters.

Jay grabbed the carton of orange juice and asked, "Ay, Rick, whatchu think about that nigga Parnell rattin' on little Vick? That shit was crazy, huh? Them niggas shoulda seen right through that little nigga's character, huh? That's why I tell them little niggas all the time a brain is a terrible thing to waste."

Rick sat back with his back reclined and his arm lapped on top of the couch. One foot rested bare on the gray Italian carpet and the other kicked up on the oversized couch separating them. He grabbed the carton of juice while watching the girl moan. He admired the fact that his dick was bigger than Jason's, considering that he was half white and all. *I must have inherited that from my momma's side of the family*, he thought to himself. He grinned and said, "Man, you know how these little niggas is these days. They ain't listening. Shit, we lucky they little asses paying attention to some a da shit we tellin 'em half the time. Niggas told that nigga Vick don't take that nigga with 'em no way. That's why we have to clean up after these lil niggas all da time." Rick guzzled the remaining orange juice in the carton.

"Never send a boy to do a man's job," Jay said as he watched his meaty dick squirt cum all in that girl's eyes and face.

"You ready for this party, boy?" Jay finished. "It's gon be ass and pussy all in that joint, feel me?"

Rick just grinned, "Yeah!" and rubbed on his hardness.

They always found themselves right there sleep on the couch after a day's work, a shower, and pizza.

CHAPTER 2

S ince their reunion over 11 years ago, they'd been celebrating each year on Jason's birthday. Today marked their 25th year on the earth. And on their turf, today made them officially O'gee's, although their young crew already considered them so. The Hilton on Hegenberger Road was the spot they'd been buying out every year since they came up. They always rented a whole floor of suites, bought the whole bar and cashed out the whole restaurant. When they pulled up to the overpacked parking lot, they parked their matching brand new SRT Hemi Chargers side by side in the reserved parking spaces. Rick had the black one and Jason had the white one. Their joints were clean too. All stock. That's just how they preferred all their whips. They both thought that decorating a car depreciated its value. But they loved loud sound systems. They stepped out in unison, dressed to kill. Literally. They stayed strapped everywhere they went. Everywhere. Jay had on the black Sean John velour sweat suit, and Rick had on the white one. They figured that they would make a theme of the black and white unity. They both had on stomach-length diamond chains with big-ass nameplate medallions. Their pinky rings were on opposite hands with the same size rocks. Their platinum Rolexes shined when the sun hit 'em. Their fitted Raider hats matched the Air Forces that they strode into the hotel in. When they reached the inside of the bar where the music was at, they both looked up at the banner and smiled. It read: "White Boy Rick, Black Boy Jay—Happy B-day!"

They slapped hands together and gave each other a love hug. They walked through the crowd of niggas and bitches receiving daps, hugs, hey's, and hi's. They went to their VIP section where their crew was at and sat down. Bottles of Moet and Dom P flourished all the tables. Everybody knew Jay and Rick didn't smoke or drink, but that didn't stop everybody else from enjoying the festivities. The whole section smelled as the pound of purple they supplied for their young'ins. Even though it was their party, they supplied every element of entertainment. Their homie Bub found a host of Bay Area talents to perform for them. They spent 65 racks on the whole little shindig.

"It's nothing," they said as usual as they toasted their cranberry doubles up.

Their section was hyphy with youngstas and hood hoes while the crowd on the floor circled around the two groups of strippers competing for the loudest applauses. The whole scene was lit and off the chain. Rick and Jay had a few chats and bump-and-grinds with a few hoes and were back in their booth chillin. Then both their heads and eyes trained on the front entrance. Little Noonie and KP came by them with astonished looks on their fat faces. They just stood there stuck and taken back. She came through the door wearing low-cut coochie huggers. Her thighs glistened in the light. Her honey-brown skin shined from the glittered flakes. Her size double D's left only the nipple to the imagination. Her Dior blouse revealed all of her golden cleavage. She had just enough ice on her neck and in her ears to accentuate her elegant femininity. Her hair was cut in a style that exposed her neck that every man wanted to taste. She had the kind of face that didn't require makeup at all. But she had just a touch of blush on to match her attire. Her lips were wet and shiny and full. She shut all the hoes down when she graced the floor. All the niggas was on her instantly. Even some of the strippers gave her a pass or two. She strolled to the bar in her stilettos and straddled the stool. Her thong leaped up the back of her shorts and both cheeks hung to each side of the seat. Back at the VIP section, all eyes were glued to her ass.

"I wish I was that seat right now," Noonie lusted.

"Nigga, I'll bust her shit out for real!" another youngin boasted.

"I'll go eighteen dumb in that thang maine," KP bragged.

Jason sat back looking to see what Rick was going to do. "So what's up, nigga? You ain't gon go say nuttin?"

Rick watched all the wolves hawking all over her. Her little section was flooded with drinks from the tricks. Rick was able to catch the next available slot next to her after she brushed a nigga off.

"I see you lookin sexy for me, huh baby?" Rick asked confidently. "Is that my birthday outfit or is it just an appetizer?"

She turned and looked at Rick, revealing all 32 of her pearly whites. Her soft brown eyes lit up at the sight of her long-lost love. Erica couldn't believe her eyes. She jumped into his arms with excitement and enthusiasm.

"Hey baby! How have you been?" she dragged out. Looking into his eyes, she continued, "I'm so glad I took my Auntie Mary's advice and came to this party. I had no idea it was y'alls party. Out of all people."

They sat and talked about old times and all the space that filled in between them. For a woman with two kids now, a person would not ever see any sign of them. Her body was flawless. They hadn't seen or heard from one another since Rick's mom got killed and he moved.

"Sorry about your mom," she consoled. "I never got a chance to tell you that."

"It's good. Everything happens for a reason. Look, you here appearing up out of nowhere. What's up wit that? You know I thought about you almost every day, girl," Rick stated, changing the subject.

Talking about the loss of his mom was still a little sensitive for him. She caught on and brushed her soft hand down his shoulder to his hands and held on tight. After Rick learned that she still was involved with her baby daddy, he was a little disappointed. But in his heart he knew she still desired him the way he did her.

Jay strolled up and broke the entranced gaze they were in. As he did, he could have sworn he saw a tear in Rick's eye. He shrugged it off. "Hey, stranger!" Jay smiled and gave Erica a brotherly hug.

"I see y'all two keeping it tight," she said.

As they conversed, Jay sensed in his gut something was different about her, but he blamed on the atmosphere. "Okay, white boy, I was just coming over to check on you. I'll holla atcha later. I'm 'bout to bounce wit this little shorty, ya dig? I see you in good hands, so I see you later, bruh. Call my room if you need me." He paused and looked at Erica seductively and finished, "For anything."

Rick laughed it off and they dapped. Jay used to always try to get Rick to share Erica with him when they were in junior high. But that was a piece he never would have dared. Erica's parents were both ministers and very strict with her. Shit. Rick barely had opportunities for himself to get a piece, let alone trying to share it.

The party dwindled down, the crowd thinned out. All the crew had their work for the night and were up in their rooms. Noonie and KP took the strippers up to their room and did it big. Rick and Erica still were stuck at the bar choppin' it up. Rick's bladder was full from all the cranberry doubles and Erica's was full of double shots of Patron. She drank like a fish all she could, since it was all paid for by the host. Rick even saw her tuck a bottle of Moët in her Coach bag. He didn't trip, though; he just was happy to see her. Rick had to catch her before she fell to the floor when they departed the stools. There was no way Rick was gonna let her drive out the parking lot that drunk. He held her up as they finally made it to Rick's suite.

Once inside the lavish room, she ran straight to the bathroom. While she flooded the commode with her insides, Rick went to the other toilet and took a long-overdue piss. He held on to the brass towel bar while he drained his bladder. He walked back out and stripped himself of his jewels and his jacket. He placed his gat under the pillow. He grabbed the remote off the mahogany night stand. He flicked on the TV and placed the remote back. He walked to the Jacuzzi in the middle of the bedroom and sitting room and started filling it with warm water. After filling the tub, he turned and wondered what was taking Erica so long in the other bathroom. He went to the door, knocked and asked, "Hey, you alright in there?"

After he got no answer, he twisted the knob and discovered that it was unlocked. He cracked the door open a bit and peeked in. What he saw bucked his eyes and surged his heart. He burst through the door and grabbed Erica by her stomach. From the back, he lifted her head out of the toilet bowl. Squeezing her stomach, he pumped the flooded water out of her lungs as she coughed back to life. Dragging her to the king-size bed, her limp arm knocked the plate of powder substance to the floor. He place her on the bed. As she lay flat on her stomach coughing, he got a cold towel out of the bathroom and covered her head with it. Seeing that she was breathing normally, he sat on the corner of the bed, watching her and thinking, *This sho ain't the same*

Erica I loved. People sho change. He wondered what else ol' Erica had been doing with herself for these past years.

Seeing that everything was going to be okay with her, he watched her snore lightly. *She probably got a hold of some bad shit or something,* he thought. He watched her ass hiked up with them shorts riding inside it and his dick jumped. Seeing her lie there made him wonder how many times this bitch dun been in a situation like this. The more he thought about it, the more disgusted he felt about Erica. He felt sorrow for her kids, though. Because of that, he spared the sexual assault from himself and from Jason, and from at least ten of his young homies. He knew that if they saw all this ass propped up like that, they wouldn't give a fuck about her, her kids and shit else. Her shit'd be violated.

As he stripped and got in the Jacuzzi he wondered, *Hmmm, would she even mind if that happened anyway?* He cut the bubbles on, leaned back, and flipped through the channels like Scarface.

*   *   *

The next morning she sat up with her back pressed against the headboard, watching TV. Her legs were crossed at the ankle and beads of shower water dripped on the half-made bed. The hotel robe wrapped around her 135-pound frame but her double D's couldn't hide under that white robe. Rick took the liberty to order two egg omelettes, waffles, sausage, bacon, wheat pancakes, toast, milk, and two pitchers of orange juice. He had been up since eight. And she finally woke up at 10:31. He gave her space to shower and unwind from last night's embarrassments. While he sat on the opposite side from her, they had eaten and had a long conversation, or should I say, she confessed all of her past and present sins to Rick.

He had learned that over the years, her dad got caught by an undercover police prostitute on the hoe stroll soliciting sex to a minor. He lost his pastorship and was booted out the pulpit. Her mom divorced him and remarried a deacon of the church who happened to be advancing passes to Erica while Mommy went shopping. One day, his built-up perverted urge took hold of him and he snuck into Erica's bed while Mommy was sleep and raped her. She told Mommy and Mommy didn't believe her and kicked her out. While out on the street, she had to go live with Judd, whom she been dating since Rick was M.I.A. Their cramped-up basement space in Judd's momma's house was not enough room for Erica, him, and the newly born bastard baby she had from the rape incident. She ended up prostituting her body late at night to take care of herself, Judd, and the baby. Judd became a part-time hustler, part-time pimp, full-time crack abuser. The monster leaped on his back and he leaped on hers. He used to beat her so much that his own momma called the police on him once. Erica, as naïve as she was at age 17, left Judd while he was in jail and ran straight to a full-time pimp named Daddy Mac.

Daddy Mac, unlike Judd, took pimpin' very seriously. It was his profession, his bread and butter. He lived, breathed, slept, ate, and ran pimpin' at its finest. When Erica climbed in Mac's Caddy on the corner of High Street and International Boulevard, all she wanted was to be led to an area where hopped-out Mexicans wouldn't drown her goals of becoming an actress. If only she'd known that once Mac snatched a hoe off the streets, they were either gonna hoe up or blow up. And he meant that. Erica's momma took little Antwon from her, which turned out to be a blessing for him and Erica. Mac recognized his young money maker as prime real estate to his stable of bitches. Mac, being a seasoned vet in the game, beat the fear of God in Erica's ass one good time, and she stayed in line and on point for three whole years. Mac had her exposed on the Internet, took her to all the casinos in Vegas and Reno, San Diego, Houston, all over the States. The only place she hadn't been auctioned off at was Mexico. Reason being was she felt she'd had enough of Mexican dicks on High Street. Mac didn't give a fuck, though. His motto was and still is, "If he can pay, he can play." Her poor little pussy been beat up with little dicks, medium dicks, and gigantic retarded-looking dicks.

Once Rick heard the story about the horse, all he could say was, "Damn!" Rick's thoughts of fucking her transformed to sympathy for her. He was glad he made a conscious decision last night. This had been the first birthday in 11 years that he didn't get no pussy. And at this point, he was glad he didn't. Mac gave her an opportunity to run when he was picked up for pimping and pandering and soliciting prostitution of a minor. She took it as a sign and left the business.

She ran into Mark at the grocery store one evening when she was staying with her Aunt Mary in San Jose. Mark had his chips up from working in the Silicon Valley at SpinCorp. She whipped some of that snapper on him and turned his square ass out. She recognized a good opportunity and sealed the deal with her other son, Mark, Jr. During her harlot stages, she developed a habit of snorting powder coke to stay up all night.

"So where'd you get that shit from last night? That sho ain't that raw I be having," Rick assured Erica. "That shit damn near took what lil' life you got left."

"I got that from some youngsta last night at the bar," she stated.

"Is that right?" Rick asked, as he wondered who could have garbage like that at his party. He rubbed his chin and continued, "That sho ain't my shit. Ima have to check that out later. Get dressed. So what's up? Where you want me to drop you at?" Rick asked, oblivious to her disrobing and dressing herself in last night's go-get-'em gear in front of him.

"Oh, that's okay, I drove myself last night. Rick, I hope I didn't scare you away from me. I used to pray that you would come back to me. Even though I have a situation right now, my heart is the same and I wouldn't want to lose you again, okay?" she pleaded while thanking him with a genuine hug and peck on the cheek. Rick didn't take kindly with the peck but he brushed it off.

CHAPTER 3

When they made it to the lobby for checkout time, Jay, Noonie, KP, and the rest of the crew were entering the lobby. Rick felt embarrassed walking with Erica. He felt like everybody knew all the things he just found out. He spoke to Jay quickly and shoved her through to the car she drove. When they reached the door of her CLK Mercedes, she pointed out little Pap as the one who sold her the bad blow. They exchanged two-way numbers and departed.

Rick sat in his Charger, crushed by the new Erica. He always had a spot in his heart reserved for her since they were torn apart by life crisis. He used to drive by her old house on 23rd and West Street in West Oakland in hopes of finding his first love. Although Rick had a host of new hoes and was getting plenty of new pussy, he always only loved Erica. At the time, she was the closest girl to have the similar characteristics of his mother. A lonely tear escaped his right eye and a tap at his driver's side window brought him back into the parking lot of the Hilton. Jay's pinky ring tapped again as Rick pressed the button for the window to roll down.

Jay knew something was wrong with his best friend. He knew Rick better than anybody. He knew something wasn't right when he saw him in the lobby. First thing he thought was what his gut said at the bar: *That bitch is a hoe. She just scheming on my dog's bread.* He saw the look on Rick's face and he knew what that look meant. It was the same look he had when he broke the news about his mom to him. His dog was hurt.

"Rick, what good, dog? What that hoe do?" Jay asked earnestly.

Rick looked him straight in the eye, lonely tear and all, and said, "Somebody been getting money outside the family." They both looked over at their group of youngstas and held a cold stare.

After Jay informed the crew to meet at the safe house on Bromly off Seminary Ave., he and Rick chopped up their next move.

"So what chu want to do?" Jay asked.

"I don't know, man. We can't keep killin' all our little niggas," Rick said as he stood with his hands crossed, leaning up against his car.

Jay knew his homie wasn't there with him mentally right now, but he didn't press for information. He knew he would tell him when the time was right. Jay leaned by him and said, "Look-a here, bruh, we ain't get this far in the game by lettin' shit like this fly over our heads, dog. And we ain't gon start now. I realize you ain't thinkin clearly right now. It musta had something to do with cha shorty last night, but don't let that shit bring down this empire we got, bruh. Suck that shit up. You can handle that shit with her ass later. But right now, we gotsta stay on top a this business, feel me?"

After hearing Jay speak the truth, Rick's blood cells filled back up in his head and he immediately showed himself snapped back.

"I know, huh, fuck that bitch, dog. She have some other shit going on, but anyway. That's some real shit. We a handle that shit at the spot in a minute. Ima see you up there in ten min."

They dapped and broke out. Jay thought as he smiled, *Lil Pap ass is out!*

Jay chose a safe house in another hood because not only did they have it on lock already, but he was always taught to not shit where you lay. They only kept guns and other ammunition there. And when you walked in the reinforced door, you'd see their arsenal first look. They had one big round table in the middle that was surrounded by 30 chairs. A picture of Al Capone was embroidered in the center of the table. It reminded them of loyalty and family. Since Jay and Rick lost the only two people they ever considered family, they built their own. Rick never knew none of his white family. So he always embraced his momma's genetics. Jay's only other family he met was his Uncle Thomas, whom he met when his pops took him to visit him in San Quentin Prison. Other than that, they really were all they got.

They stood while everybody else sat at the round table. The only other two people who stood up were Noonie and KP. Noonie and KP were twins. Identical. If you didn't know KP had a birthmark on his upper right shoulder, you really wouldn't be able to tell the difference. After being around them two for so many years, Rick and Jay knew them apart from their voices. Other than that, both brown-skinned, black-eyed, shoulder-length-dred fat boys would be mistakable. They were big for their age of 19. They earned their trust when they both didn't rat out Rick and Jay when they saw them smoke Big Hen years ago. When the police rounded up everybody in the hood that day, Rick and Jay were the number one suspects. The police showed Noonie and KP photos of the two from their foster parents. And Noonie and KP cussed the pigs out. At their ages of 13 years old, that was a rarity. Rick and Jay took them under their wing ever since. Their mom smoked a gang of coke too, and they never knew their hopped-out dad. The last thing they ever heard of him was that he was a shot caller for the BGF in Folsom Prison. So far as they knew, Jay and Rick were their only family. They stood at the door holding two Russian AK's and ready for a command. They were up on what the meeting was about already. So they stood ready to squeeze. Everybody sat attentive, listening to Rick spill the message.

"This crew is about unity, trust. It's about respect and love for your fellow family member. We are your family." He eyed the whole crew and spread his arms out as if he was giving out a group hug. "It's about loyalty to each other. We're a team. One man can't win the game alone. It's like when Michael Jordan goes up for the slam, and they win the game." He went up for an imaginary slam. "He couldn't have gotten the ball from himself." He eyed Jay. "He got an assist from Scotty Pippen." Jay passed an imaginary ball to Rick. "Scotty got a pass from Horace, Horace got a pass from Robert Horry, and so on." He pointed to the crew.

The whole crew shook their heads in agreement, even Pap. Pap, unaware that Rick was standing behind him, kept slapping the table in agreement. Pap, aka Mexican Pap, moved to the hood three years ago with his family from East LA. He befriended Lil Larry by sleeping with his sister and giving Larry free weed to smoke. He thought he was smooth with the ladies and eased his way off the porch in Rhonda's coochie. Rhonda was the neighborhood runner (neighborhood hoe). She ran the streets and her mouth. She let Pap know what was going on and who was doing what. Pap took the invite and used his persuasive mouthpiece and free weed to end up grinding on the block for Jay. Since Jay was fucking Pap's momma, Josephine, when Mr. Sanchez went to work, Pap was a cool little youngin. Earlier, Jay and Rick decided that they weren't going to kill the youngin because of that reason. But they sho as hell was going to give 'em something to remember the rules by.

Rick slipped out the rope from his sleeve and quickly wrapped it around Pap's neck. Instinct made Pap grab for his neck, but Jay already had the metal pipe out, slapping Pap in his stomach, making his hands drop back down. While Rick pulled, his legs came from under him, kicking wildly. The chair slid back and Pap landed on his back flat on the floor. The rest of the crew watched in horrified amazement Jay repeatedly slapped and slapped Pap's ribs and stomach. Rick tightened the rope around Pap's neck so tight his whole head turned red.

"Where you get that bad shit, huh?!" Rick demanded.

Pap gurgled out painful words that nobody could understand. Rick squeezed tighter, so tight that even he turned red. He looked like he turned into a totally different person. Jay had stopped beating the boy out of mercy for his momma, but Rick kept choking him. Pap started vibrating ferociously and his eyes rolled in the back of his head. Jay saw that Rick was still squeezing the rope tighter and rushed over and pulled Rick off the boy.

Jay turned to Pap and started slapping his face in attempts to revive the boy. He commanded a youngsta to bring some water and splashed it on Pap's face. Jay pounded on his chest and turned him over on his stomach. Pap threw up a ton of spaghetti-looking contents. He choked and coughed hysterically while he wheezed himself back to life. Jay dripped perspiration while Pap dripped blood. Blood and vomit were all over the hardwood floor and table.

Noonie and KP stood smiling menacingly looking down at an inch-away-from-death Pap. Jay looked at the other youngstas' scared-to-death faces. He turned and saw Rick sitting in the same position on his ass, holding the rope he just damn near strangled Pap to death with. He sat there panting and smiling with a devilish and evil sinister mug on his face. Jay didn't say a word, he just shook his head and smiled at his partna as if to say, 'Nigga, you crazier than a mutha fucka' to him.

CHAPTER 4

Rain poured down mercilessly on the window pane and Jason plunged his dick mercilessly into Mrs. Josephine Sanchez's vagina from the back. Mrs. Sanchez was not a fat woman but she was overly thick. Her ass, when it was bent over, looked like two big yellow beach balls together. She had one of them headboards that detached from the bed. That made it less noisy so her other three kids wouldn't hear Jay thrashing their momma's pussy relentlessly. Her husband worked swing shift at the Port of Oakland as a loader. Jay knew to be at her door at 30 minutes after 12 midnight. Mrs. Sanchez had a thing for black men. Every hood she moved to, she had her pick of the litter. She'd always tell her best friend, Loraine, that black men were more passionate lovers. And the way Jay coaxed her ass proved her right again.

"Oh, oh, ay Papi, sí, sí, I feel it, I feel it."

Jay flipped her over and put his dick head on her clit and massaged it. He sucked on her big brown nipples like a newborn baby.

Mrs. Sanchez was a beautiful woman in her mid-thirties, but she could easily pass for twenty-something. Over the years their adulterous behavior landed them in a secret love affair. After what little Pap told her from his hospital bed, Jay promised her that he would find the gang who did it. Jay really developed feelings for her over the years, and that was the only reason why Pap was still living today. Pap was lucky to only end up with three broken ribs and a bruised esophagus.

Mrs. Sanchez grabbed Jay's ass and pulled him into her wet walls. She held on real tight as she came all over his shaft for the sixth time. Jay kept going with circular motions and pulling in and out while kissing Mrs. Sanchez vigorously. His 165-pound chiseled oil-black frame drenched her 150-pound body. If it wasn't for her loyalty to her kids, she would do anything Jay asked. She looked at Jay with love-filled pupils and kissed his nipple with her tongue. That was Jay's spot and she knew it. Jay started pumping faster and she squeezed harder. Her pussy muscle gripped Jay hard, making his thrust tighter and more addictive. The mass of his dick filled with blood as he pumped one last time and exploded all his lustful infidelity juices into her receptive pleasure cave. Mrs. Sanchez had her tubes tied after her fourth baby four years ago. So Jay had been getting good caliente pussy for three years without the worry of anything.

Jay lay on his back, feeling guilty for what he and Rick did to her son, but he knew that that was the game. And to play the game, you've got to leave your emotions at home. She rubbed his chest and kissed his ears. Her hands felt good and warm on his body. Her big, warm thighs rubbed all on his and he was back at attention. Her hand found its way to her black hard pleasure pole and she gripped it at the base and stroked it once. She curled under the cover and placed her hot mouth over the head. She bobbed and slurped and went to work on it like a professional head doctor. Jay moaned and twitched and let his hands find her moisture. He fit two fingers in it and then three. She gyrated on his hand and he pumped in her mouth. They both reached their climax and loud moans brought them to two-times ecstasy together. Their twain became one flesh the entire early morning.

*   *   *

That same morning, Rick sat in the driver seat of his old-school Malibu, listening to Too Short's "Short Pimpin." Any minute little Vick would be walking out the front door of the police department in downtown Oakland. Seeing all these police cars and people in suits walking around was making Rick nervous. He thought a number of times to leave and let Vick catch a cab back. But how gangsta would that be to the little homie? An hour and 11 minutes later, little Vick bopped out, swinging his dreds from side to side. Since young Parnell wasn't able to testify against him and they didn't have no weapons, all they had was hearsay and that was inadmissible in court. The judge had to let him go free.

Little Vick was a tall, skinny nigga with caramel skin with black eyes. He came from a good family but he chose to do opposite of what Mom and Dad preached to him. He smoked a gang of weed and he joked a lot, but he loved to bust his tool. Rick and Jay used him as a torpedo when they wanted to blow something or somebody up. Rick hit the horn and flagged Vick to his car. Vick hopped in and Rick peeled off.

"What's poppin, big dog?" Vick smiled while giving Rick daps.

"Ah, nothing, little daddy, how ya feel? You cool, man?" Rick asked while driving down Broadway towards MacArthur.

He looked at Vick and smiled that his young homie beat that shit. Rick took a liking to Vick. He knew Vick was a real soldier. He knew niggas like Vick were hard to come by. He dug in his pocket and pulled out a fist full of cash and handed it to Vick.

"Here ya go, young dog. You been gone for six months, you gonna need to catch up on some shit. That should get you through a few." He looked at Vick's clothes and smirked out, "First, we about to hit up the mall and bring you back, though, feel me?" Rick stated.

"Hell yeah, dog, I feel ya. I know one thing, though, I'm hungry den a mutha fuckin hostage. That county food ain't cool for a nigga like me. Oh yeah, one love for handling that shit for a nigga, big bruh. That was my bad. I should'a listened from the get."

"It's good, don't trip. We holla about that later, though. As for now, first things first." Rick headed up to the MB Mall, where they shopped all afternoon.

Vick bought all the latest shoes and all the latest Sean Jean fits. Before he left on his six-month vacation paid for by the state, Sean Jean and Jordans were all he sported. All the girls loved him for his swagger. They went and ate at McDonald's in the mall and Vick had his favorite burger, a Quarter Pounder with cheese. Vick reminded Rick so much of himself when he was his age. They swapped stories about the little Pap incident and Vick listened intently. He liked little Pap and felt kind of bad for him. He was glad that he was able to escape with his life. Vick told Rick about what some niggas was in jail lying on they dick about how many hoes they fucked. Some niggas even lied and said they had a platinum helicopter. That brought laughs between the two.

But one question Rick had to ask that probed his mind since the day he found out that young Parnell had snitched. One question his curiosity would not let rest. One he had to wait until he was face to face with Vick to ask. Because he wouldn't ask over the phone and he wanted to hear from the horse's mouth.

"What happened that night I sent you to old boy?"

CHAPTER 5

S he reluctantly guided his love muscle into her warm saliva. Her soup coolers massaged his sensitive peak. After the beating, she found herself once again enslaved to his subjection. In her mind, she felt that she had no choice but to submit totally to his will. His strong hoe checkers gripped the back of her head. Her hair entangled his hand so tightly that her brain felt as if it was going to be pulled out the back of her scalp. Her left eye was closed and unable to see the grin on his menacing face. Her clothes were scattered all over the room from what had been an unsuccessful attempt to ward off her assailant. All the particles were ripped and shredded from his claws. A lone tear escaped her good eye as she accepted his forceful blows to the back of her throat from his oversized tool. He watched his possession from an elevated view with bloodshot eyes. His perm swung as he began pounding her throat harder, making her gag. Too scared to stop for fear of frustrating him, making him open up another can of whoop-ass on her, Erica swallowed the puke that came up her esophagus.

Mac had let her go to the party to come up on a prospect. He knew that it was gonna be some dough in the building. So he sent his number-one money-maker. Erica truly didn't know that it was her junior high sweetheart's party. And once Rick busted her in the bathroom with another demon, she really felt out of bounds. Everything she had confessed about her past was true, all except Mac being in jail. She really did have a baby daddy named Mark, and they were once in love. All up until Mark found out she was a prostitute. He took Mark Jr. and kicked Erica back on the streets. There on High Street, she ran back into Mac. Yeah, she had truly given up her profession as a hooker when she bubbled on Mark. Mac had let her out of his sight once. And that once was one too many. Once Mac patrolled

High Street one extra lap before he took it to his stable, there she was. Freezing, and drenched with water, standing in the exact same spot where he found her four years ago. And that was one-and-a-half years ago today. Erica angered Mac when she stayed gone all night and only came back with $300. He would not have had that if she didn't pit stop at one of her regulars that morning she left the hotel with Rick.

Mac forced himself to pull out of Erica's mouth before he skeeted all his aggression in it. He took both his hands and grabbed Erica by her shoulders and threw her back onto the bed. He stood there looking at her like a pitch-black devil. She panted and lay up on her elbows. Mac grabbed Erica's left ankle and flipped her over on her stomach like she was a rag doll. He jumped up on the bed between her legs. He reached over to the plate of raw coke, scooped some in his hand, and shoved it up his nose. He snorted like a pig and took the leftover and massaged it on the tip of his dick. Then he pressed close to the black eye of Erica's behind and pushed in slow. Erica propped her ass up and took all of Mac's 12-inch dick in her with ease.

After finishing up with Erica, Mac got dressed without a shower in his black suit and black cowboy boots and black cowboy hat. His one silver tooth smiled at Erica as she lay there coked out on the bed, naked. Mac went into his living room where the other girls were. They all came to attention when they saw Mac. He whispered to his bottom bitch, Monica, to keep an eye on Erica and do not let her leave. He had other business to take care of. Mac left his stable and hopped in his '66 Cadillac Eldorado with the stacked headlights and chandelier with the dome lights on the side and fifth wheel in the back. He headed across the Bay Bridge towards his track where pussy was always bargained.

Erica lay up in the bed, dropping silent tears. She wouldn't dare give those other bitches the satisfaction of hearing her sob. She thought about how much she hated Mac and the revenge she had brewing for him. She felt like getting up and beating the shit out of that bitch Joyce for snickering at her when she came back. She smiled at the reunion of her lost love. She wished she could have just stayed with him and never come back. She wondered what her life would have turned out to be if they were never separated by life's crisis. She felt her eye and let out a light "Ahhh!" She rubbed her body's soreness from top to bottom gently. Then she curled in a knot in desperate need of the coke that Mac left for her on the table. She thought how much she wanted Rick back and how much he despised drug users. She knew she would have to quit cold turkey and that would be hard, especially after 2½ years of abuse. She smelled the feces under the cover and got up towards the master bedroom shower. When she saw herself, she muttered, "Come on, Erica, you better than this." She then ran the shower warm and washed herself thoroughly. She squatted down and squeezed all that cum out of her ass and pussy that Mac deposited.

After drying herself off, she sat on the corner of the bed, looking around the room at all the scattered clothing. She saw her two-way pager and thought of calling Rick. Then she looked at the powder on the nightstand by the window. Both looked tempting. The powder to escape her nightmare of reality and the window to escape her prison of prostitution. She looked at the pager and thought of a better way to escape all three, the third being Mac. She wanted to punish him and make him feel all the pain she'd been through, and all the humiliation as well. She herself was too weak to even contest the 6'3", 240-pound black gorilla. There was only one way to handle it. She finished oiling herself up and grabbed some of her lodge clothes out of the closet. She knew Mac's bottom bitch would be keeping a close eye on her now. So she flipped on the TV and picked up her cellular and dialed the number.

CHAPTER 6

J ay saw Mrs. Mathis pulling out of her driveway when he stepped out of Mrs. Sanchez's door that morning.

"Humph." Jay smiled mischievously at the old lady.

She turned up her nose as she rolled her dark, wrinkled eyes and sped off. She always seemed to catch Jay at the same time every time he visited Mrs. Sanchez three or four times a week. Jay noticed she forgot to lock her gate this time. He took the liberty to go shut it for her nosey ass. Then a plan hit him over the head. The sun was barely peeking from the east. Mrs. Mathis lived alone and only got infrequent visits from her daughter once a week every Sunday. Mrs. Mathis's husband died of a heart attack five years ago and Mrs. Mathis hit it big with his life insurance claim. She still kept her job at the caregivers facility where she'd been a nurse for 28 years. Her life only consisted of going to work, going to church on Sunday with her 40-year-old daughter, coming home, and having Neighborhood Watch meetings, which she was president of. Then she'd sit up in her window and watch all the youngins sell tons of coke, weed, and heroin all day and night. She even called the police and had a few people sent away for drug trafficking. A couple of youngstas harassed her a few times already, but it proved to be no effect on the 65-year-old woman.

Jay looked up and down the block. He saw some scattered dope fiends looking for cream. He reminded himself to make sure he had some youngstas on this early morning shift. Jay walked to the back of Mrs. Mathis's house. He climbed the back porch and peeked in the window. Through the kitchen, everything was still and very neat. With one swift kick, he kicked the back door off the hinges. He waited at the door to listen for an alarm, but he heard none. He stepped on the tile of the kitchen floor and the Pine Sol assaulted his nostrils.

"Damn, Mrs. Mathis," he mumbled.

Jay passed through the kitchen and through the dining room. Her dinette set looked straight out of a magazine. He thought it to be a big difference from the house he just left out of three houses down. He never would even imagine places like this even in this hood. He peeked in the china cabinet and saw all the unique pieces. Her oak table looked like it had never been eaten on. Her table shone with a sparkle. It almost pained Jay to think of what he was about to do. He went through the living room of Italian leather brown couches. His wet Nikes left mud marks on the beige carpet.

He started searching the house for valuables. He was tempted to call for a moving U-Haul truck and haul off all her shit. But he wanted to be out of there soon. He searched her bedroom, looking for nothing in particular. He stumbled over her jewelry case and found a bunch of old rings and necklaces, pearls, and rubies. He stuffed all of it in his pockets and commenced his search. While in the closet, he saw a carry-out safe. He picked it up and brought it out. He looked back in and saw a 12-gauge shotgun standing in the corner. He smiled at the thought of her old ass bussing that thing. He grabbed that too. He went into the kitchen and found some Hefty garbage bags. He came back in the bedroom and threw everything in the bag. He grabbed all her clothes out of the closet and dumped them in the middle of the floor of the living room. She had furs and minks, and leathers and silks. Her wardrobe was expensive. Then Jay grabbed the safe and all that he'd placed inside the bag and took them to the back porch. He sat them down and went to the utility shed, where he found two bottles of lighter fluid by the barbeque pit. He took them inside the house and soaked the pile of clothes and everywhere else in the house. He emptied the bottles and threw them on top of the clothes. He grabbed some paper bags out of the garbage can and burned them on the stove. They caught flame and almost burnt his hand as he threw it onto the pile of clothes. Making a mad dash, he almost forgot to grab the safe and the bag. The entire place caught flame rapidly and smoldered.

He walked out front casually with the bag in hand. As he popped his trunk in front of Mrs. Sanchez's house, Mr. Sanchez was just arriving. Jay placed everything in his trunk and opened his door and climbed in. Mr. Sanchez glanced at Jay and gave him an innocent nod with his lunch box in hand. Jay nodded back with a smile as if to say, 'Thanks for leaving that good-ass pussy unattended at night, sucka.' Jay sped off just as the flames started leaping out the roof of Mrs. Mathis's house. Mr. Sanchez didn't notice the flames and went inside his house to his awaiting wife and kids.

As Jay made the right on Rudsdale, he saw dope fiend Bill coming up the block with his rag and windshield wiper spray. Bill tried to flag Jay down but Jay waved him off. He got on his cell phone and called Noonie.

"A, what's crackin, little daddy?" Jay spoke. "Ya'll don't go on the spot right now or probably none today."

"Why, what's up, dawg?" Noonie questioned.

"Just don't. It ain't cool right now. Call everybody else and let them know too. I'll holla at chu later, aight, one." Jay ended the call without getting a further response.

He sped to the house in Hayward and rushed in the house and dumped all the contents on the kitchen floor. Nina came out the back, fully dressed and ready for work. Nina was Jay's girlfriend for two years. They met at the gym and had been working out together ever since. Nina ain't the finest woman on the earth, but sure ain't the ugliest either. Her body made up for any discrepancies. Her booty looked extra plump in any pair of pants or sweats she worked. Her thighs were not full but they fit her five-foot frame. She sported her hair pinned back in a ponytail wherever she was at. Jay fell in love with her attitude. She didn't drink or smoke and she was faithful to God. Jay usually came and hid his dirt in her house when she wasn't home. Even though he paid all the bills, he still gave her respect. When he heard her coming down the hall, he hurried and placed the bag over the pile and spun around.

"Hey, baby, I thought I heard you come in." She came with arms open, wearing her work suit and a smile.

He eased toward her past the counter and received his hugs and kisses. He felt like shit kissing her with Mrs. Sanchez's pussy juices on him.

"Baby, what chu doing still here, ain't chu late?"

"Yeah, but I was on my way out now. I just wanted to change for the weather, it's cold out there." She gave Jay one more kiss and brushed past.

"Jay, baby, you ain't gotsta keep being slick; I know what you're doing out there in them streets. I'm not stupid. I just want you to be careful, baby. I love you and I don't want nothing to happen to you." She walked back over to him and kissed him. "I love you, Jason."

Jay felt another pound of guilt smash him. "I love you too, Nina." He meant it. She left out the door and he rushed back to the pile.

It took him two hours to pry that safe open with a screwdriver. But when he opened it, he was rewarded with stacks of bills. He smiled when he counted the money. The old lady had stacked up 150 racks. He tucked the 12-gauge under the living room couch. He knew Nina wouldn't wear those jewels but he tucked them away anyway. He took the money and peeled Nina off 10 racks and put it under her pillow. One thing Nina didn't turn down—well, two: (1) Jason's dick and (2) Jason's money. He put the other 140 racks in his safe and went and showered and got dressed. He sat down on the couch and flipped the TV on. The next thing he knew the TV was watching him snore.

He woke up to the sounds of his phone vibrating and the sirens from the noon news. Dennis Richmond explained the details of the single-home fire on the TV, and KP explained it over the phone. Jay smiled at the fact that nobody knew who started the fire in the hood and there weren't any suspects to the apparent arson. When Jay got off the phone, he took in a couple more minutes of rest.

"You niggas betta get down or get laid down." Little Vick had the Mack 90 trained on all the youngins at the dice game. They all lay there in the prone position, eyes to the ground.

"Empty out them niggas' pockets," he commanded a hyphy crew member.

As the cadet did what he was told, Vick kept the chopper on the bodies. After the bag was full of all the day's hustle and all the earning and losses of the victims, they all filed back into the van. Since Vick had been home from beating that murder, he had been feeling untouchable.

"Nigga, this our town, we run this mutha fucka, feel me?" Vick yelled as the black caravan sped down Market Street.

The hyphy crew had robbed almost every turf in West Oakland that weekend. Two spots they robbed left two niggas dead and one wounded. Their last stollo had to be left at the old man's park with bullet holes in it from a gang that retaliated. But that didn't stop the hyphy boys. The hyphy boys don't give a fuck.

"I'm gonna show you little niggas what's up. Ima show you niggas what it's like to be a soldier. Ima show y'all what my big homies Rick and Jay did for me when I was a young nigga. Ima let chall know what this shit about, ya dig?!" Vick shouted.

The other five youngins in the back were attentive with their eyes glared up front at Vick. Noonie was driving like an expert driver from NASCAR. He grinned, passing the blunt back to Vick. The entire inside of the van reeked of purple haze. Noonie already knew what Vick had in mind because Jay and Rick had done the same thing to him and KP when they were younger. So now the grooming was on their most trusted young soldiers.

"I'm bout to head to the east, my nigga," Noonie told Vick.

The five youngstas in the back were bouncing around in the back, swaying to the music 106 KMEL provided. The van didn't have a CD player and Vick complained about it every time the latest R&B song came on. Luckily, it was Rap now at the moment. They passed blunts and drink around while Noonie rode the 580 Freeway toward East Oakland. The commercial came on about the bestselling author TBone from Caliber Publishing releasing his latest book. He was having a book signing at Eastmont Mall. Vick went crazy,

"See, little nigga, that's how you do it. Ya hear that?" he said, referring to the radio. "That nigga TBone straight out the street for real, nigga. Been to the pen and everything. I read all that nigga books when I was locked up. We gone have to slide by there later on today."

"That's real," Noonie said.

They exited the freeway off the MacArthur maze. They rode past Lake Merritt.

"Oooh, look at that ass!" one youngsta named Ray Ray shouted.

"Damn!" another stated. Baby girl was stacked nice, running around the lake in her biker shorts and sports bra.

The scene was lovely. Women filed around in clusters on the grass on the sides. Couples enjoyed the fresh sky after a rainy night. Men walked around the man-made lake trying to scout out their mate for the afternoon. Traffic was thick. Afternoon bustas were in their whips stuntin'. Police cruisers patrolled the traffic. Noonie straighten up and drove the stollo like a modest citizen. But that still did not stop the police officers from eyeing the van full of young black males. A motorcycle officer was standing by the stoplight with the speed gun pointed. Noonie dropped the speedometer by 2 miles per hour. The van crept past the white officer with the distinctive nostrils. The van passed by and he got a good strong whiff of the purple. He jumped on his Harley Davidson and sped off in pursuit of the van.

"Man, that dick head jumped on us, man!" Noonie yelled. "He right behind us!" The motor dick was directly behind the van with its berries on.

"Damn, homie, you can't pull over. You do that and we all gone be through with money," Vick explained as he gripped the assault rifle.

The little hyphy boys in the back had the look of fear running all through their eyes. Noonie made a left turn on Lake Shore Drive and put the pedal to the metal. The van leaped into full throttle and sped past all the cars in traffic.

"Smash, smash!" Vick yelled out.

Noonie maneuvered the van through traffic at top speed with the motor dick heavy in pursuit. He was on his walkie calling for backup. Noonie banked a right, then an immediate right and raced through the hills. Each turn he turned, he just couldn't lose the motor dick.

"Man, fuck!" Vick shouted.

Noonie kept the pedal to the floor harder and leaped over the speed bumps in the street. No matter what he did, he just couldn't elude the motor dick.

"Fuck!" a voice shouted in the back seat.

The back window flew out from little Ray Ray's bullets hitting it, causing it to bust open. Glass shattered to the ground and bullets barely missed the pursuing cop. The motorcycle quickly slowed and pushed to the side of a parked car. The officer, recognizing his fate, leaped off his motor bike and tumbled to the ground, rolling over. Noonie turned another right and headed down to the flatlands.

"Yeah! That's what I'm talkin' bout, boy! Fuck them police, they ass can get it too!" Vick was excited.

He hopped around in the passenger seat, grilling all 32 gold teeth. Little Ray Ray still held the spent smoking pistol aimed at the back window frame. The other youngins sat there holding their still-cold guns, explaining to Vick what they were going to do and would have done. Vick gave them the deaf ear and passed Ray Ray the blunt.

"Now see, you little niggas!" Vick was spitting as a matter of fact. "That's what we was gonna see if we had some soldiers or what wit us in this shit. Before it's over wit, all you little niggas gone get a body under y'all belt, and that's real! Cuz we don't want no rudy poot ass niggas on this team, feel me?" he spat to the youngins as Noonie swooshed the van through the back streets.

They made it to their underground parking lot at the end of the mall where their legit rented four-door gray Pathfinder was parked.

They cleaned the van out and wiped it down, then piled in the Nissan and spun out.

The book signing was in another hour, so Noonie drove around to the other side of the mall and parked. They decided to walk around the mall until TBone came. They took their beanie caps off and pulled their black hoodies off. They all exited the vehicle dressed in white T's and black jeans. Two people out the crew had blue jeans on. But overall, they still looked one alike. Noonie and Vick draped themselves with today's jewelry takes so they stood out from the rest. Vick passed Ray Ray a white-gold stomach-length chain with a diamond cross on it. He felt that he was the one who deserved to look better than them other youngins since he put in work today. Ray smiled with appreciation.

Inside, the mall was packed with shoppers and patrons. The hyphy boys' swagger swung through the mall like a pack of hungry pit bulls. No one stood in their way. Vick had his 9 mm Ruger in his waistband and he felt invincible. They bopped their way to the second floor and walked around. From the top they could see the first floor. There was a pack of females walking, doing their female fashions of hyphy. Extension braids swung back and forth, a lot of loud gossip exchanged, and their spot thrown and claimed. It fascinated Noonie to see how girls acted and tried to be so much like dudes.

"Hey, little mamma, what it do, y'all live or what?" Noonie shouted. He hung over the railing and his dreds hung too. Six years of growth was long enough.

"Yeah, we live, nigga. We out here, ain't we?" a young yellowbone thick one yelled up.

"I see them jeans fittin you nice too. Where y'all bout to be?" Noonie spat.

"We-a be around, y'all a see us. What's your name?" she asked.

"Noonie. What's yours?" he asked.

"Tamika." She smiled. Noonie grilled her with gold fronts. For Noonie to be a big nigga, he was considerably handsome; all the hyphy boys were.

"Where ya'll from?" Vick asked the skinny dark one. She had the littlest mini skirt with the smallest blouse with the loudest mouth. But her character revealed strength and Vick like that.

"We from North Oakland, where y'all from?" she asked.

"We be them hyphy boys, you ain't know?" little Ray Ray yelled out.

The girls went into a frenzy. The boys started bouncing around shaking their dreds and the girls shaking their extensions. They conversed loudly and moved on.

CHAPTER 8

The mall flourished now in anticipation of the author TBone. He was inconspicuous when he arrived so that no one knew he was there until he was sitting at his seat in the middle of the lower level floor. There were banners of his publishing company hanging around the mall; also his latest new release. He sat there with a black fitted Raiders hat, black loose-fitting T-shirt with his label on it, and black loose-fitting slacks. He was caramel-colored with dark, wavy hair with a goatee. You would have to be up on him to see his brown eyes through his specs. From just looking at him, you would think he was just a square in his early thirties.

"Man, we came around here to see this square-ass nigga?" Rell spat. "Fuck that nigga."

"See, little nigga, that's what I'm talking bout. You can't always judge a book by its cover. That nigga got more history in the town than all us put together," Vick said, referring to the crew. "That nigga just got his chips up and did something with 'em. And he a flatten yo little ass quick too, nigga, so don't get it twisted."

As they approached the crowd of mostly girls and women, they noticed the little female crew they were getting at earlier getting their books signed. Vick noticed Bone still had it when it came to the ladies too. He also noticed this thug-ass grimmer-looking nigga about to snake Bone too. As the other crew members hollered at the ladies and got their book signed too, Vick broke off and gained TBone's trust when he caught the dude off guard as he was about to clock Bone from behind. Vick put the butt of his gun to dude's head so fast, no one saw it. Then he tried to hit dude again, but Bone was already on him. Dude was a good 245 pounds but he was no match to the experienced 235-pound muscled Bone. Bone gave the boy so many quick 1-2's, the boy was out off his feet. Vick was about to blast dude right in the mall, but Bone grabbed the youngin and calmed him down. Bone searched the dude while security ran up late and cuffed dude up. Bone tucked dude's .38 revolver before security hauled dude off. The crowd applauded Vick for his heroism.

TBone finished signing the rest of the books and handed Vick the last one. He and Vick went and sat and ate at the Chinese restaurant.

"Good looking out on that situation earlier, youngin," Bone continued. "What's yo name, young homie?"

"My name Vick, and that was nothing, man. I saw dude about to creep on you, so I had to do something. I read all your books when I was locked up. And dug your style."

"That's cool. Check this, though, I hope you learned something while you was in there, though. I peeped you was about to flatten the youngsta in front of all them people. Especially them women. It's already bad enough we got bitch-ass niggas tellin', but a broad'll tell even faster. You feel me? You gotta be smart, youngsta. It's a time and a place for everything."

Vick listened attentively and soaked up as much game as he could from the O.G. homie. Bone gave Vick a lot of insight about the game, some stuff Vick already knew, but he still listened. Come to find out, TBone grew up in the same hood as Vick that the hyphy boys terrorized daily.

"I heard what happened to that old lady Mrs. Mathis's house too. Some stuff can be avoided, though."

"Oh yeah, how is that? She was always too nosey though."

"You gotta elevate your mind, V. All whoever done that had to do was get inside of her mind, start being nice to her. Start being respectful to her, you know. Kill 'er with kindness. A good word go a lot further than a bullet. You feel me? She's a woman; her head can easily be manipulated."

"I feel you, I feel you."

Bone gave Vick one of his business cards and told Vick to call him up if he needed a job or anything. As Bone dapped Vick and left, Noonie and the other hyphy boys came over. They had the group of girls with them.

"What up, bruh?" Noonie asked as he slapped five with Vick. "I seen you over here in a lesson with the teacher so I kept the crew back. But o'girl been really buggin' the shit out me about chu, though." Noonie tilted his head to the skinny dark girl waiting for Noonie to go finish talking to Tamika so she could advance.

"Yeah, dude real, though," Vick smiled. "So little mamma on ya boy, huh?"

"Like a yellow jacket at a family barbeque, boy," Noonie grinned.

Shawnie and her eager boldness approached Vick as Noonie spun off. Up close, she was finer and fuller than Vick thought at first. She was petite, yes, but full in her figure. She and Vick were about the same size and height. Perfect match. She was a couple of inches shorter and a shade or two darker than Vick, but he liked that. She liked Vick's keen eye for danger and his help in saving her number one author. She told Vick about how much her mom loved TBone's picture on the back of his books and all of his exotic and erotic fuck scenes. That sparked another conversation and Vick's interest in her own sexual fantasies. After a few details, they decided to hook up a bit later. They switched numbers and both crews departed. Vick took a look back at Shawnie and saw that she was eyeing him the same. They both smiled at one another as Vick and the crew exited the mall.

Inside the car, Vick took a look at TBone's business card, tucked it back in his pocket, then looked through the rearview mirror at the hyphy crew passing blunts around and decided to give the boys a pass on what would have been tonight's mission. He had other plans.

*   *   *

The Buick Regal's windows were foggy like a cold winter night. From the front of the house, you couldn't see over the hedges that stood 12 feet tall surrounding the house, blocking its view. The sun had set at 9 p.m. and all the neighbors always called it an early evening whether it was summer, spring, winter, and fall. Living in Stockton, California, people had more fun in the house anyway. If Vick didn't want this sweet pussy so bad, he probably would have thought twice on the commute from Oakland. But he had few regrets. Shawnie's panties hung on the rearview, her pants flung over the front seat, and her blouse raised over her neck, revealing her chocolate firm B-cups. Vick's hands were grabbing and caressing them as he nibbled in her ear from the doggy style position.

"I thought about you all day." He pushed inside her moistures and had to restrain himself from wilding out. And as young as he was, Vick pushed his 10-inch pole inside Shawnie's fresh tight squeeze. She also felt in her soul the more than just a fuck from Vick.

She moaned out, "I thought about you too."

They both felt each other's core vibration. Vick took slow, long, deep strokes. Her ass was a perfect arch and just enough mass for Vick's body to fit like a connecting piece to a puzzle. Her scent was natural and enticing. Vick craved her more with each stroke. He hadn't been inside no pussy this good since he'd been home. Actually, he never had any this good ever. She fit his shaft like a tight grip of a fist. She tried to keep up with his slow, passionate pace, but she couldn't. She started bucking faster and faster as she felt her own liquids about to flow. The more she bucked, the harder he pressed, making him stretch further inside her walls. His fluids reached the tip of his nozzle just as hers broke like a dam. They both let out moans of grunts from their bowels. He erupted his loins all inside her and she all on him. The smell of sex filled the air and soaked in the interior. Vick's own pants leg hung to the side and his white T was wet with sex juices at the bottom. His sweat dripped on the curve of her lower back into a small puddle. They disengaged and sat back on the seat listening to KBLX, quiet storm. Vick held her in his arms, kissing her full lips. He licked the sweat off her forehead and she rubbed and held on his chiseled frame.

"Ah," Vick said.

"Yes," she replied softly.

"You took my feelings somewhere else, little ma. I know it might sound corny, but it's real."

"You took mine too. It's like I felt your soul inside me. It's kinda hard to explain. I know I haven't had sex in a while, but still," she said sincerely.

"What's a while?" Vick asked playfully while massaging her dark nipples. He felt the urge pulsate through his loins again and he answered it. She felt the passion go through her soul and she responded to every light touch as she answered incoherently.

"Thirteen months, after my last boyfriend."

Vick continued to send charges of ecstasy through her body and arouse his own. He laid her back and pulled her to him and asked one more question.

"What time you have to go in?"

There were no more words spoken. Their bodies entangled into a unit. They made love right there in front of Shawnie's mom's house for four straight hours. The car danced to the rhythm of their bodies and Vick and Shawnie danced to the quiet storm.

CHAPTER 9

Rick rode in silence through East Oakland. International Boulevard was packed for a Sunday morning. The engine to his Malibu purred through the dual exhaust system. His window was rolled down and he took in the good early morning breeze. Families escorted themselves through the traffic on their way to local assemblies. Caravans of Raider fans rode the streets, representing their #1 team of Oakland. Rick thought of going to the game himself as he and Jay usually did when they played at home. But today, he wasn't feeling it. He passed by High Street and saw the young prostitutes out there selling their bodies. He thought of Erica and how she explained her life to him. He shook his head and wondered how she was doing. He wondered if he should call her up, since she hadn't called him yet.

He picked up his phone and noticed it was turned off. *Damn,* Rick thought. He thought of all the money he'd been missing as he turned it on. He forgot he had turned it off when he was at the hospital visiting little Pap. Little Pap was scared to see Rick that morning. Surprised and scared. For one, he thought Rick was coming to finish him off. And two, he was just plain spooked now. All Rick wanted was the information on who he was getting that bunk dope from.

"That's it," Rick asked. Rick promised him he was going to take care of him and that he apologized for the incident. Rick had a way with words that would soothe a person.

"I stole it from my dad," Pap told him.

Rick couldn't believe that shit. Out of all this time, Pap's dad turned out to be the man in East L.A. So now, not only did Rick feel fucked up about what he did to Pap, he had to get to know Pap's dad. On top of that was the information that Vick gave him on the other business.

Rick's phone beeped from the missed calls and message feature. He looked down at the screen and saw the missed number. When he looked back up, he had to apply his brake hard. Immediately he slid 15 or 20 feet. When the car stopped, he was inches away from the back bumper of a family in a station wagon. They stood at the light on Seminary in a panic, looking at an almost fatal accident. The black family counted another blessing. The female passenger threw a cross in the air and her husband sped off when the light turned green. Rick also counted a blessing that he didn't tear up his fresh old-school Malibu. He would have been pissed off at that ass.

He met Jay at the Denny's on Hegenberger Road, like they always did on Sundays. Jay hadn't been to their apartment in a couple of days. Rick spent the weekend chilling in the house, watching college ball and thinking. Jay was already in a booth when Rick arrived.

"What's crackin'?" Jay asked.

"Ah, nothing, bruh, just ain't seen you in a couple. I found out some real shit, though. You know that dude? Oh boy? Lil Vick, you feel me?"

"Yeah, yeah," Jay agreed. "Yeah, I member. Yeah, what's up wit it?"

"Wrong dude. Oh boy cousin got everythang. Dude told Vick before you," Rick uttered. There were a few people in the restaurant but not quite packed yet. A couple of hours from now, then it would be filled with after-church members and family.

They conversed over their meals and OJ for a few minutes. Rick filled Jay in on all the details of the next move. This move was important. Once they got what dude's cousin got and dude's cousin out their way, they'd be set. Dude and his cousin controlled a great big chunk of the town and were very major factors in Rick and Jay's advancement. But when Vick went and hit dude, dude's cousin got away with the entire product. Now he's not slippin'. But Rick did the homework on their whole get-down already and he knew exactly how to get to dude.

Rick told Jay about Pap's dad and Jay said, "What? You fuckin kiddin me? All this fuckin time Pablo been right on our fuckin block? This shit is unbelievable. I'm fuckin Pablo Sanchez's wife. The notorious fuckin Pablo Sanchez's wife? Plus we damn near killed that fuckin dude's son? What the fuck? Now what we gon do?" He looked at Rick incredulously.

"What you gon do is, since you fuckin Pablo wife, is get all the info you can from the bitch. If you gotta fake it, then fake it. But you do it. You feel me? Do what it takes. But whatever you do, don't be fuckin stupid. I wish I woulda been fuckin the bitch at this point, but she like dark meat, and my white dick don't match my black soul. Cuz yo ass liable to fuck up shit," Rick said.

"Naw, Ima handle it. I got mommy wrapped," Jay bragged. He held his privates as he flagged for the waitress to bring the check.

"When yo ass coming home, nigga? At least call and let me know what's up wit chu." Rick stated his concern.

Jay told him about the lick he pulled on old lady Mathis and where he tucked the dough.

"So yo ass burnt the house down. No wonder all those cops been jackin up everybody. Good thing you didn't tell nobody you did it. How Nina doing anyway? You need to gon lock that down and quit playin formal. That's a good broad right there."

"Aw, nigga, that shit already on lock. Besides, she be wanting me to go to church wit her and all that. And I ain't ready for that yet," Jay said.

"Well, you probably need it now after old Mathis," Rick laughed. Jay cringed. Rick finished, "One thing for sho, you either gone walk in or gon be carried in one day."

The check came and Rick paid. Jay left the tip. Outside the diner they talked at Jay's Charger.

"Bruh, you alright, blood?" Jay asked. "Lately you been kinda somewhere else. Ever since you seen Erica."

"Man, she really been lost without me, man." Rick stood there for a minute, then sat on the hood and spilt it out to Jay what she told him. After hearing all that, he felt a little bad for her too because he knew she was better than that. But he felt even worse for Rick because he knew how Rick felt about her. He used to get sick of listening to Rick's stories about how much he missed her and how much he loved her. He knew Rick hadn't even had a steady relationship with a woman on the account of hoping that Erica would come to him one day.

"Bruh, I wish it was something I could do to rewind the time," Jay said. "But we can just keep the faith, bruh, and if the love is real on the other side, y'all a be back together by faith."

"Thanks, bruh, I needed to hear that," Rick said. "I luv you, bruh."

"I luv you too, bruh."

They gave each other hugs and departed.

They would usually go get a quick workout in at the gym. But Jay wanted to go spend some time with Nina, and Rick opted to go to his mother's grave site and spend some time with her. Rick was depressed from all the incidents that encompassed him about. And every time he felt depression, he went and talked to his momma. She was the only one who understood him and who could make him feel better. Even though he couldn't see her, he could still feel her presence and hear her voice. He remembered times he would talk to her with his feeling when she was alive and she always had the answer. Never once was she wrong.

At the grave site, he parked outside the "Evergreen Pastures" and walked in. There were two other people visiting their deceased loved ones on the other side. He knew exactly where his mother's plot was. He'd been there plenty of times over the past years. She had a headstone implanted inside the ground above her. Rick removed the old red roses and placed the new ones in the urn. He unfolded his lawn chair and sat it beside her like he always did.

He felt that she understood how much he liked to stay clean and he smiled. No matter how many times he came here, he always got jittery. And he always sobbed first. Rick always reflected on how much he needed her when he was growing up. He sent a thank-you card with a thousand-dollar money order in it every Christmas to her old job, because it was her employer who gave her a good burial service. Rick spoke to his mother about everything. He looked at it as him placing his confession on an altar. When God took Rick's momma away from him, he always wondered why and how God could do that to him.

After talking to his mom for a couple of hours, he stood to leave and after folding the chair, he took one of the roses out his mom's urn and walked two plots over, removed the old one out and placed the new in, and said thanks to the only dad he'd ever known. Mr. Jason

Darren Hill Sr. had been the only father figure he knew. It was Jason Sr. who stepped in and filled the void when Jason's mom ran out on him. Jason knew all about it. It made him and Rick feel even more like real brothers then. Seeing Mr. Hill brought a smile to Rick's face because he knew that Mr. Hill loved his momma as he did. And he knew that his mother loved him also. It had gotten to where Rick even started calling Jason Sr. Dad and Pops.

Rick walked to his car and put the chair away. When he sat down to leave, he heard his phone beep. He checked the missed call log and saw his missed calls from the same 408 area code. He couldn't remember anybody from that area offhand. So he wondered. He went ahead and called it back. After two rings, Erica answered, sobbing and sniffling and sounding hysterically gibberish.

"Calm down, calm down," Rick stated. "What happened, where you at? Ima come get chu."

Erica told him where she was and stayed on the phone with him to ease her mind while she told him everything that happened to her. Rick blew his mom and stepdad a kiss and pulled off. Erica was the only girl Rick's mom ever liked. The only one to ever get her approval for her son to date. Rick valued that dearly. He thought of that as he exited the cemetery.

CHAPTER 10

Mac came through the door looking like a black panther, the cat. He reeked of the Crown Royal he'd been drinking all night and day while he watched his hoes get that dough. He had to leave his track in a hurry with the 12 racks he had on him. It was mandatory that his hoes brought him at least a "G" apiece every day. Mac was old school. He believed in stacking every penny. He had 20 different bitches, all races. He usually worked 12 hoes a night 7 days a week. Mac preferred to not spend a dime on anything new but food and powder. He had a lot of dough, he was just hella bootsy. But his pimp hand was strong. And bitches liked that. Mac came in giving orders to his bottom bitch.

"Take these hoes back out there and bring them other bitches back, ya dig? I be back out there in a little while, ya hear? Them fuckin police out there sweatin a pimp and my bitches out there can't see they daddy get jacked up. So bring them bitches back with cha, ya hear?"

Monica couldn't move fast enough before Mac's backhand came smacking her upside the back of her head. The other hoes scurried around fixing themselves up and getting ready speedily. Mac looked at his watch and then back at Monica and the hoes. Before Mac counted down to 3, all the hoes were out the door. He then peeked in on Erica, who was sitting up with an ice pack on her eye, watching TV out of her good eye. He still saw the fear in her when he shut the door.

Mac went to the kitchen and pulled the refrigerator out of position. He peeled the wallpaper off the wall and opened his safe. Mac never locked his safe because in a crunch situation, like when he went to jail and needed immediate bail, he was able to call and tell Monica to go get it. Even though he and Monica were legally married and been together for 20 years, she still couldn't remember shit. Especially a fucking easy-ass safe combination. *Dumb-ass bitch*, Mac thought. It was she who turned Mac on to pimpin when she hoe'd up for him to pay their rent a long time ago. That was why Mac still loved her. He wouldn't admit that he loved a hoe around a hoe, or to a hoe, but she knew it.

Mac placed the G's on top of the others and smiled the silver-tooth smile. He shut it and placed the refrigerator back in its place. He stood and grabbed his already hard dick and looked to the room where Erica was. He licked his skanky tongue on his black lips and strolled toward the room.

*   *   *

When Rick entered the house, Erica was sitting on the couch staring blankly at the walls. She'd left the door ajar for Rick when she told him to hurry over. Rick walked up cautiously.

"Erica, Erica," he called out.

He walked up to her after no answer. He placed his hands around her wrist gently. He then grabbed the bloody blade out of her hand and stuck it in his pocket. Erica sat there, eyes bulged, fully drenched in blood. At first, Rick thought she'd sliced her wrist. But when he let her wrist go, he saw no open gashes. She sat, breathing chest-fulls of air.

Rick assessed the situation quickly. He followed the pathway of blood to the other room and bloody doorknob. Rick took a part of his shirt and opened the door. When he saw the scene, he had to hold his breath to keep the contents down in his stomach. Mac lay spread out on the bed with his pants down to his ankles. His dick was in his mouth. His stomach was sliced open and his intestines spilled out. From his severed dick, the shaft was dripping the remainder of blood out of it. The whole floor was soaked with blood. The smell was unbearable. Rick turned around to Erica, ran to her, grabbed her by her underarms, and pulled her up. He wasted no time. He stripped a cover off the couch and wrapped Erica in it. He grabbed her cell phone, two-way, and everything else he saw that might have been hers.

As he pulled Erica out the door, Erica pointed to the kitchen. Oblivious to her hand, Rick put his arm around her, shut the door behind them, put Erica in the car, and sped off.

Rick couldn't believe what just happened. Out of all things that he could have walked into, that was the last thing he expected. He kept glancing over at a distraught Erica in the passenger seat. She sat there looking straight ahead and trembling from the cold blood on her. Rick drove straight to the Hilton and rented a room. He took Erica in through the back door so no one would see her. He didn't know what was going on but he didn't trust Erica, not one bit, to have her know where any of his spots were.

In the room, Erica stood naked in the shower while warm water ran over her entire body. Blood ran down the drain while she sobbed, washing herself off. Rick piled all her bloodstained clothes into the cover she wore around her. He washed the blade off he had in his pocket. He disassembled it and put it in the pile also. He then tied it all in a knot and left it inside the bathroom. He glanced up and caught a glimpse of Erica's bodacious body as she washed herself. He also shook his head at all that wasted life.

"I'll be in the other room, alright?" he said.

"Uh-huh," she said.

He pulled the door shut as he backed out and went and sat on the bed. He flicked through the channels until he saw Angela Bassett acting Tina Turner on stage performing with Lawrence Fishbourne as Ike Turner. He stopped it there and leaned back. He thought of his mamma and then shook his head as he thought, *How could a punk-ass nigga just take advantage of a weaker woman?* He looked at the bathroom door and thought of Erica's eye being purple when he saw her. Then he tried to imagine his scenario of what might have happened.

The water in the bathroom shut off and then minutes later Erica emerged from the bathroom in one of the complimentary robes. Besides the purple eye, she looked good wet. Lust was far from Rick's mind. Erica's too. She sat across from Rick in the single chair at the table. She placed her hands on her knees and started talking.

"Rick, first I want to thank you for being there when I needed you. Thank you." Rick just sat there looking at her attentively. She continued, "It's a lot I have to tell you."

Rick cut her off. "Start from the beginning."

She finished, "There's a lot of stuff I omitted from the first story. Most of it was true, though. Anyway, I do still love you, that's a fact." Rick sat there unmoved. "Well, what just happened back there was years of built-up abuse and frustration," she said while rubbing her knees.

"You sure you weren't high?" Rick asked sarcastically.

"No—well, yeah, a little, but I swear to you I just couldn't take it no more. Then when he came in drunk and he slapped me around, and had the audacity to make me suck his filthy-ass dick, I snapped." She rubbed her temples and ran her fingers through her hair. "I grabbed my razor out my pocket and held it real tight as I waited until his dick was all the way hard and..." she sobbed.

"That's okay, E, I got chu. We gon get through it. You gon stay here for a while until we figure this out. But if I catch you with any more dope or drink around you or in your system, I'm gone and you can go back to the dogs. I hope you feel where I'm coming from 'cause I'm too real for that bullshit," Rick stated.

"I promise, Rick, I promise. I don't ever want to lose you again," Erica expressed.

She grabbed Rick tighter but Rick just released himself from her and sat back down at the TV. Although Rick felt disgusted with Erica's trash, Rick couldn't help the fact that he still loved Erica very much. He still knew that he would do anything for her. "One man's trash is definitely the next man's treasure."

Rick thought love was one thing but expression of love was another. She was going to have to do something to prove to Rick that she still loved him. And Rick knew exactly what it was. She couldn't have come back to Rick at a better time. Rick sat back, thinking. He thought of how his plan would come together. The things that young Vick told him had him in deep thought. Not only was it about dude's cousin getting away and them taking over. Rick saw a bigger picture than that. Rick had wanted to get out of the game for the past three years now. He'd actually been waiting for the right opportunity to make it happen. Although he and Jay had a few million between them, Rick had always felt like he was missing something. An empty void in his life. Something that he'd been envious of Jay for having these past few years: a woman.

Rick watched Erica sit and sob with her face inside her hands and he wondered if she'd be able to really quit. He leaned back and flipped through the channels on the TV. While the TV watched Rick, Rick watched Erica. Reserved in wonder, mixed in hope and doubt and pity.

CHAPTER 11

J ason sat on the block like a general commanding his troops to knock
off the dope. He sat across the street on a milk crate while dope fiend
Bill gave his Charger an outside detail. He didn't want the inside done
because he had his dope stashed in the dashboard and he didn't want
Bill to sniff it out. Bill was an old-school baller who fell off 20 years ago.
He used to have the exact same hood on lock. The only difference was
his time was back in the early '80's/late '70's. It was cool to snort dope
and smoke grimmies (weed and coke in a joint). One serious drought
came and Bill couldn't find a gram of coke anywhere. He ended up
selling off his toys one at a time until one day he looked up and only
had his house he bought and his habit. His wife left him for another
baller and he took his habit to another level—freebase. The only reason
he kept his house was for his hope of his three kids to come see him
whenever their momma came back to California so they'd know where
he was at. Oh, plus he let the crew cook up dope, keep guns, and stay
there sometimes.

Jay and Rick wouldn't allow anybody to post up in front of his
house because it might burn the spot haven up. Jay picked up his carton
of orange juice and took a swig. He looked up and down the block and
admired all the traffic. Their block got weed, coke, powder, crack, hop,
and ecstasy. Their spot was known as "the one-stop shop." Bill was
just about finished his detail. Jay was just about tired of Bill grinding
his teeth too. That was what Bill did. Bill had fingers like frog feet, his
crusty frame was always cruddy, and he ground his teeth.

"Jay, it sho look good out here since you woke them youngins' game
up and tell 'em to get out here and get this early mornin' money." He
spit out his inch gap in his mouth.

"Yeah, it do," Jays said. "That hop money real good and them fiends gotta have that first before anything else. If not, they ass a damn near die for real in three days."

Dill ground his teeth.

"To each his own, but I'm sho glad I ain't choose to go that route, boy. It ain't no get-back on that shit. I was always scared a that shit. You can catch that shit fuckin round with the wrong needle."

Jay watched his only father figure since his dad got killed Armorall his tires up. "Bill, you need to gon get chu yo own detail shop open up, you raw fo real. You see how all these niggas come lookin fo you all the time? You be missing some real dough," Jay stated.

Bill ground his teeth. "I am one day, you gon be surprised at the ol' man. You know I ain't always been like this," Bill bragged as he spilled into one of his umpteenth-time telling his ballin history. Jay always listened too. Jay didn't listen because he liked hearing the story. He listened because he didn't want to take Bill's inspiration away. Jay had much respect for Bill. He knew how Bill's heart was. Bill had been a witness to plenty of Jay's terrorism. Plus, Jay knew that Bill was just a good dude, period. Real genuine. He let Jay and Rick live with him when they ran from the foster home. Bill never asked them for nothing except for them to support his habit of smoking coke.

While Bill applied oil to the last tire, Jay commanded a knock to his youngins across the street. As he did so, he saw Mr. and Mrs. Sanchez drive by and turn into their driveway. He watched Mr. Sanchez park and they exited the vehicle. Jay thought he sure didn't want to kill the man, but he would if things didn't go right.

Mr. Sanchez went to the back door of the car and opened it up. Mrs. Sanchez got out the passenger side door and acted as if she didn't even see Jay. Jay mumbled, "We gon see how you act tonight, bitch." And he smiled. Mr. Sanchez helped Pap out the back seat. He was still in pain but he'd live. Jay saw the youngin and he felt sympathy for the kid. The kid saw Jay and nodded. Jay felt an amount of respect for the kid for keeping it solid. Mr. Sanchez looked to Jay and gave him a head nod too. Jay acknowledged them both with a wave. The Sanchez family headed in the house.

Bill's grinding teeth brought Jay back to Bill standing beside him. Jay knew what he wanted now, so he gave a youngin across the street a head nod and sent Bill over to get paid. Jay adjusted his .45 Desert Eagle around in his waistband for comfort, propped his leg up on the crate, and rested his elbow on his knee. He looked to his right and saw the burnt-up house that now had a couple of youngins occupying it holding assault rifles. He smiled demonically and thought that things were much better now since old lady Mathis was gone.

He looked to his left and saw more traffic. As the traffic got closer, he saw a foreign car. He knew the model to be a coupe leading the line. The car got closer and inched up behind Jay's Charger. The other three cars pulled behind it. Jay had his hand already on his .45 ready to squeeze at the first sight of a weapon. The youngins in the house were already aiming the assault rifles at the cars. Bill's house was now empty of its storage of weapons. And all the youngins had formed a line down the sidewalk across from the cars. KP and another youngin named Kareem had joined Jay at his side. Even Bill came up, grinding his teeth, holding a mini 14.

The driver's door swung open and the passenger door too. The driver stepped his gators on the concrete and shut the door of the Bentley. The passenger door stayed opened and a fine-ass Asian bitch stood behind it. She watched the driver strut over in his ¾-inch black mink matching his shoes and his car. The other three cars' occupants exited the vehicles at the same time, all brandishing weapons. Dude in the mink held up his hand for them to chill and Jay did the same thing to his crew. He walked up to Jay with a smile and both hands raised to air.

"I come in peace, my brother, chill."

Jay recognized him already and was millimeters away from pumping his mink coat with slugs and sending him to go meet his cousin. But Jay chilled. He was curious as to wonder why this nigga would risk his life coming here like this and what the fuck did he want.

"Can we talk?" he asked.

"Talk about what?" Jay asked.

"Business, business, brother, always business," he stated.

"I ain't got no business wit chu, homie," Jay expressed

Homeboy, which is dude's cousin. Dude being Big Reg, who young Vick murked. The cousin being Donnell, but everybody called him Dubb. He was known as a scary nigga who didn't want no problems with anybody. All he knew how to do was get money. Big Reg was the rider. And by Dubb being Big Reg's cousin, everybody respected him for that. Now that Big Reg was gone, Dubb was in charge of the crew because he had all the work. He stutter-stepped over to Jay and held his hand out. Jay reluctantly took his hand and they walked off to the side to talk.

"So what's up, man?" Jay asked.

"Jay man, how long do you want this war to go on, man?"

Jay didn't answer him.

"When Reg was living, it was crazy. Y'all hit us, we hit y'all, and on and on. When y'all caught us slippin and got cuzzo, y'all kilt the head. I was lucky to get away. But I ain't never been the gangsta type a nigga. That was Reg. I always told 'em he can't mix war with getting money. Nobody eat."

Jay just listened.

"Plus, with it all being behind numbers and territory, I knew it could be a better solution. That's why I'm here. Jay man, think, we out here killin each other and the MEC getting all the real money. We ain't getting nothing but the crumbs. Even if it's a mill or two, it still don't compare to what the MEC gettin. Shit, they got poppy fields and coke fields as far as the eye can see, man. They need us. So while it's good, we might as well get all we deserve out here, feel me?"

Jay nodded and still didn't speak, Jay still didn't trust shit he was saying, but he felt some parts of it. Jay wished Rick was here to make this decision. He was the thinker in shit. Dubb continued.

"Yeah, y'all smacked my cousin and when y'all did that, that shit hurt, but that was a wake-up call for me. In honor of my cousin, I'm willing to squash our side of this funk and work with y'all, if y'all can supply my demand. When cuzzo died, the connect died with him. He didn't even let me know who his connect was. All we need is thirty bricks a month." He watched Jay's expression.

Jay cocked his head to the side and one eyebrow raised. Jay and Rick were only moving 20 bricks a month themselves. But this was what they were looking for. This was what the funk was all about anyway. Even though Jay's and Rick's connect was barely able to cover their order monthly, he still couldn't pass on this opportunity. He said fuck it; he was going to make it work somehow.

"So if we decide to go along with this, y'all gon roll with the price settin at 500 a zone and y'all gon squash y'all side of the funk?" Jay asked.

"Man, like I said, my word is bond. This been going on for too long already," Dubb said. "And this opportunity is gravy for everybody. I'm about the money, Jay, so let's get it, man."

Jay and Dubb shook hands, gave each other a light hug, and turned to their crews, who stood ready. They both smiled and gave the hand signals for everybody to lower their weapons. They made each member of their crew throw up the peace sign to each other. They switched numbers and Dubb jumped in his Bentley and smashed off with his crew in tow and the FBI. And just like that, the most deadly funk of Oakland, California, was over—or was it?

CHAPTER 12

O l' school Ben-K sat at the Oakland BART station waiting for his ride to arrive. He was restless from his six-hour ride on the plane from Illinois to the San Francisco airport, his 15-minute cab ride to the SF BART station, his 30-minute train ride from the SF BART station to the Oakland Coliseum BART station—and oh, his 10-year stint in the Feds. So you can imagine he was a little anxious. Before he left he was a notorious head buster for his nephew. Word was he flattened about 50 heads in his lifetime. He smoked a lot of coke and he always got caught slipping by the police with a weapon on him. He robbed so many people in the town that whoever saw him would automatically either give him something for free or suffer being stripped of everything. He didn't give a fuck who you were, where you were from, what you'd done, or who your people were. He stayed ready for war. He didn't have any kids, so after his sister died of a crack overdose, he took his nephew in and raised him in the streets. When he was free, he'd terrorize all the ballers and kill all those who opposed him. The coward was glad, but the heavy hitters were mad when he got picked up and took a deal for 10 years as a career criminal just for having a knife in his possession.

Ben-K was lucky the good Lord rescued him in a couple of ways. One way he was bought by every baller with a little heart. It was only a matter of time until somebody collected that dough. And two, he was smoked out so bad that he was 60 pounds underweight. Six months to the house, he found out his nephew got killed and he went crazy. Not crazy as in out of his mind, but mad. He was furious. He sat in his cell the whole day and cried. He literally snapped a dude's arm because he was mocked for crying over his nephew.

As soon as he got out, he called his girl Silvia and arranged to be picked up. Silvia rode with Ben-K wherever he went and whatever he did, and she kept it solid with him through his 10-year jolt too. She may have smoked up 10 keys of coke while he was gone and tricked a little, but she stood with Ben. She managed to keep a little raggedy Ford Escort for transportation. She was one of those female smokers who tried to hold on to whatever poise and dignity the crack monster didn't steal over the years.

She pulled up and found Ben-killa looking every bit of the stocky 5'10" caramel-skinned Caesar cut with waves, wearing tan khakis and a tan button-up, handsome man she knew 30 years ago. She felt embarrassed when he hopped in with his release box on his lap and didn't kiss her. He just spoke.

"What's up, Sil? What the fuck took you so long?" he growled.

He looked her over and turned back to the view out the window. He didn't give a fuck how Silvia looked now at the moment. He still loved her and he understood what crack does to people. Plus he knew Silvia's heart and what she still was capable of looking like. But Silvia thought he was judging her and she felt indignant.

"Well, welcome home. I made you a big dinner; it's waiting for you at the house."

She managed a smile. Her dark skin shined and her hair was pinned up. Her prewashed clothes were clean and she tried to present herself as best she could in her 110-pound frame. But Ben saw right through the façade. He really wasn't tripping off Silvia or crack. He made his mind up six months ago that he wasn't going to use crack anymore. He had revenge and judgment on his mind. Money and murder. Kidnapping and robbery. He wanted the mutha fucka who was responsible for killing his nephew. And he planned to make their ass pay.

While he was away, he studied Christianity: forgive and forget; turn the other cheek; vengeance is mine, says the Lord. He was a Bible scholar. But he had to sit his Bible down to settle this matter himself. He looked at Silvia and realized how he was treating her after all she'd done for him, and he softened up.

"I'm sorry, baby," he said softly as he kissed her on the lips.

A tear rolled down her cheek and she headed to the house. They made it to her shabby little apartment in the deep East Oakland. She kept the same apartment she had since before Ben got locked up. It was located on 100th and MacArthur, right across from the rundown motels right on the turf of some local thugs. Ben-K viewed the youngsters out there as they pulled up to the gate. First thing he thought was how he was going to extort their young asses and their boss. A couple of them were already at the car, trying to serve Silvia. She was so embarrassed when she waved them off, and when they saw the look on Ben-K's face.

"Sorry about that, O-G," one of them apologized as they backed off.

One of them noticed the box in Ben-K's arms and stated, "Welcome home, O-G."

Once inside the desolate apartment building, Ben-K felt he was in another world. Silvia may have smoked a gang of coke, but she sure as hell kept a clean house. The brown leather couches may have been a little worn and the carpet old and run over, but it was clean. She had wood tables with the glass in the middle. There was a mantel that bordered around the walls. It had pictures all around on it. She caught Ben-K holding one and rubbing the face as if it was a person.

"I miss him too, Benjamin," Silvia stated.

She was the only person Ben-K allowed to get away with using his government name besides the government.

"He was the only person who would come and check on me and who would give me money for you. He would always say he can't wait until his uncle came home."

She walked over to him and put her bony hands around him. They both stood staring at a picture of Big Reg and Ben-K standing by Reg's '69 drop Cougar. Ben-K was a lot thinner then. He reflected back to that very day and he smirked.

He placed the picture back and turned to Silvia. He looked her in her eyes and said, "Thanks for everything, Sil. You mean the world to me. You and my nephew is all I had. I'm gon have to go back out there, ya know."

She didn't respond. She already knew how he was thinking. She just shook her head and squeezed him real tight. "Just be careful, baby. And you already know I'm with you for whatever. That was my heart too."

They went into the kitchen and gazed at the table full of food. She cooked enough food for an entire family and it was just them two. Ben-K looked and said, "How I'm gon eat all this food, Sil?"

She smiled and said, "You gon eat enough and I'm gon eat more than enough." She expressed herself with her hands and eyes up and down her body. "I have more than enough space for it."

His smile faded and he said, "Baby, you gon have to kick that monkey off. Baby, this a new day. God don't want us tearing our body down. That's His temple, you gon have to make space for Him to clean it out."

She shook her head as if she already knew it. "I know Benjamin, I know, and I am. I'm with you for however long you want me to be, you know that, so let's start putting the weight back on with this food before it gets cold."

They sat at the table and Ben-K said grace, and they ate as much of the full-course meal as they could. They got so full that they couldn't do anything else but sit in the living room cuddled up, watching TV. Ben-K couldn't help but keep glancing up at his nephew's picture. All he could think about was how he would strike down with great vengeance on who did that to Reg. He kept telling Reg over and over about his punk-ass cousin and how he didn't need any fake-ass niggas around him. But he knew Reg was just happy to have some blood around him, regardless of how scary they were. Ben shook off the thought and Silvia. Then he went to the back room and prayed.

Ben-K raised his nephew after his sister Joyce overdosed on crack. He always felt guilty, like he owed her his life because it was his crack pipe they shared that she took her last pull out of. If his other sister, Betty, wasn't so uppity, he'd have confided in her. But he knew that would be useless. She packed up and moved to Georgia because she thought he and Joyce were the devil. She even left her punk-ass son with one of her churchgoing friends to raise because he went to a good school. So Ben had to smother that guilt by being a parent to Joyce's child and committing a host of murders. And when he went in and out of prison, what Silvia couldn't instill in Reg, the streets did the rest.

CHAPTER 13

"**H**e did what?" Rick questioned through his cellular phone. "Who that nigga think he is? Man, you shoulda been called me. Even though that's solving half the problem right now, but in the future, that shit gon blow up in our face. That messed off my whole plan I had, damn! Anyway, man, can't change it now. Your word is your word and that's what it's gon be," Rick stated as he sat at the table of the hotel counting the day's pickups.

Jay listened to Rick's spill on the other end and he knew by the sound that Rick was pissed. He was pissed at himself too for not letting Rick make that decision. Then to let them niggas come to the turf deep like that and didn't squeeze. Jay sat there mad as hell. He wanted to go shoot a nigga just to ease the pain. But he searched his mind for a reasonable defense until he found the only one he could muster up.

"Nigga, where yo ass been any fuckin way? If yo ass was here you woulda been able to support some shit. I had to handle all this shit lately by my motha fuckin self," Jay spat.

He and Rick debated back and forth for about an hour about who was right and who was wrong. Jay was so busy running his mouth that he didn't even see the Crown Victoria pull up, take his picture, and leave. The only thing that made him turn around was the sound of Bill grinding his teeth. He turned around to face a wide-eyed Bill staring at him. He was so pissed off that he didn't realized how he answered Bill.

"What!" he asked.

Bill flinched a bit from Jay's gripe. "Ahhh, uh, I was just gon tell you about the 5-0 that passed you and took your picture." Bill paused. "They was plainclothes."

What did Bill have to say that for? Jay heard that and froze with his ear glued to the phone. Rick's shouts drummed in his ear.

"What the fuck he just say?!" Rick yelled. "Hell fuckin naw, I know he just didn't say what I thought he said. Man!" *Click.* Rick hung up the phone without saying another word.

Jay stood there with the phone plastered to his hand. Bill stood there wondering if he might have done the right thing by telling Jay. He knew it was right, though. But he didn't know how Jay felt because Jay's expression showed another emotion. Bill ground his teeth.

"Jay, it's hot, man, gon shut down early and get up outta here. Them dudes didn't look nice. And it sure didn't look like they was gon be playin fair either. When they want chu, they come get chu. And they don't care how they gotsta do it either. I seen my homie get took down by them bastards a while back. Trust me, shut down till it cool off." Bill gave Jay good, clean, sound advice, just like he always did.

But like always, in one ear and out the other, Jay insisted on doing him. "Nigga, fuck them police. 5-0 always come through here. That ain't the first time them crackers probably came through." Jay spun and walked away toward where little Vick and Noonie and the rest of the hyphy crew were posted.

"Yeah, I know," Bill stated to Jay's back. "But them was the other people, though."

Jay kept moving. Bill ground his teeth, cursed, and wished that Rick was around lately. He turned with his window cleaning supplies and went on his mission.

Neither Rick nor Jay had been to the penitentiary before. Both of them had been to the county before, though. But that was only for some tickets. They had escaped some lifelong terms by never leaving any evidence to prosecute them. And they both detested those interrogation rooms. Jay's wits had always kept them pitching rocks at the penitentiary. Rick's sharp decisions had always saved Jay and himself.

*   *   *

Rick sat there thinking, sitting in the chair at the table with his legs crossed with stacks of cash on the table. The TV was watching him and so was Erica as she sat propped up on the king-size bed with plates and trays of room service around her. Rick had her under surveillance for a couple weeks now. He'd been closely observing her and watching her withdrawal from her habit. She made it through the initial stage without dying, thanks to Rick's close monitoring and cold baths he'd been giving her. The maids had to come change the sheets and covers three times in one day, but the bathroom had been off limits to them. When Rick left to pick up his money off the street, he took all her clothes and underwear with him. He took all those bloody clothes and burned them up.

As she watched him through tired eyes, she reminisced on their younger relationship. She remembered how serious Rick was even back then. A smile surfaced on her face, then she said, "You had that same look when you thought little Robert Washington was trying to flirt with me. And when the lady in the cafeteria mistakenly gave you a diet tray."

Rick smiled a bit as he remembered those exact incidents. "Oh, you still remember that, huh?"

"Hell yeah," she said. "I remember every single moment we ever spent together. I cherished them back then and I cherish the memories now. You shouldn't be too over-serious all the time. Life is too short."

"That's just me, though," Rick defended. "And that's just how life is—it's serious! You slip up once and it's all over. You play too much and you end up being played. I can't afford that shit," he emphasized.

She edged to the corner of the bed and sat there with all of nature exposed. Then she stood up, put her hands on his shoulders, and started massaging him. "You have a lot of tension, daddy; you want to talk about it?"

Her gentle caress felt good and it had Rick relaxing and loosening up. Her soft hands had Rick really in a tranquil state. Her clean scent aroused the sleeping giant inside his pants. The whole time they'd been at the hotel they hadn't had sex, not one time. But that still wasn't enough for Rick to pillow talk his business with no woman. That was something he just didn't do. With his head bobbing, he answered, "Naw, it's good. It ain't nothing that can't be handled."

He left it at that and she didn't pry nor probe to persist. Her hands found their way to his chest and worked gently around his nipples, sending more sensitive charges though his body. She loved the more developed, chiseled frame of the more adult man Rick had become. She glided her hands to his eight-pack and breathed her warm, sweet breath through his ear. Her eye had healed up well, all but a light bruise. But now at least she could see. Rick's body shivered for more of her seduction.

She maneuvered her way around to his pants and knelt down and unzipped his Girbauds. His hard stick sprang forth and her mouth enveloped it. She worked Rick over like the professional she was. Erica, being the experienced veteran she was, knew exactly where to maintain her focus because it only took 10 or 12 at the most deep throat and tip of the head of Rick's dick strokes from Erica. Rick felt himself tense up and tingle all over and one of the best feelings to ever take hold of him. He breathed deeply in and out and he gripped Erica's ears and head into his palms. His face reddened and his eyes rolled in the back of his head. He sighed loudly out his mouth as the jewels gushed out a family tree worth of sperm into Erica's mouth. Rick was so caught up in the feeling he heard himself sigh out, "I love you." He doubted that Erica heard him, but at the moment he didn't care.

Erica finished quenching her thirst and she eased up off her knees. As she stood up, her moisture dripped out on the floor. She looked down at Rick; his eyes were still closed and his head was leaned back. She looked at him and she whispered, "I love you too." And at that moment Erica felt something inside her that had been missing for a long time. Something that all the sex she'd ever had couldn't fill for her or compare to. She felt love. A tear escaped her eye and she turned and went and lay in the bed.

Rick's eyes opened to see Erica curled under the cover with her back facing him. He felt tingly all over. His insides felt drained of liquid and filled with passion. He felt like he was whole again. He felt the feeling he'd been missing for years now. He felt his reason, his purpose, and his desire to will to do. He stood and he stripped himself of all his clothes and jewelry. Then he slipped under cover with his lost love and snuggled into her body warmth. They just lay there, connected like two Lego pieces, stuck.

No matter how many lovers or sex partners one might have, sex is only just sex unless it's with the one you love. Erica was just a hollow shell and all her sex partners were just her sex partners. The closest she'd come to even having something close to companionship was with her kid's father, Mark. But even then, her true heart wasn't in it. But now, she felt complete again, she felt real. And when they made love, it was just that—real.

CHAPTER 14

Knock, knock, knock! The hard whacks on the door startled Dubb from his early morning fuck session he ritually gave Meggin, his wife. Her white-pale skin and his light-dark skin looked illuminated with its sweat. Dubb kept pounding Meggin from the back until he finished his husbandly duty. When he finished and grabbed his robe, he left Meggin to her shower before work as he rushed to the front door. *Knock, knock, knock!* Again the door sounded.

"Who the fuck is it! This shit better be important coming to my house this damn early in the morning!" Dubb yelled through the door.

Dubb lived in a cul-de-sac in a nice quiet neighborhood in San Leandro. Only his most trusted crew members knew where he lived. Sometimes when they needed work, they would swing by and snatch up the couple of emergency keys Dubb kept at the house. When Dubb snatched open the door, ready to grill one of his workers out, his face dropped to the floor in full amazement. All the false manhood evaporated. All the tuff sounds and hard talk turned into cowardly gestures when he saw his momma's brother standing at the door. Dubb always knew that Ben knew his true heart. But what he didn't know was when Ben-K was getting out of jail.

Ben-K brushed right past Dubb and stopped in the center of the living room. Dubb closed the door and turned around to meet Ben-K's fist on his chin. Dubb buckled to the floor hard. His 225-pound, six-foot frame melted like Silly Putty. Ben-K kept his tyrant of terror storming on poor Dubb. Dubb was already knocked out, but that didn't matter. Ben was mad and pissed off at how Dubb allowed somebody to get close enough to smoke Reg and nobody paid the price for it yet. Half of the crew had already left on that account alone too. It was any day that Dubb was subject to a robbery murder and betrayal anyway.

Ben-K was beating and stomping Dubb so bad and viciously that he didn't hear the shower water stop. The screams of Meggin's high-pitched voice snapped Ben-K out of his brutal assault. He turned to see a naked, white, gorgeous brunette standing in the hallway screaming in horror. He stood up and rushed swiftly to where she was too slow turning to run. He grabbed her by her hair, yanking her backward to his grab. His arm wrapped around her thin throat in a sleeper hold. He squeezed once hard enough to cut off her air supply to her brain. She fell limp in his arms with no restraint.

Dubb woke up to an excruciating headache, partial vision, the taste of blood in his mouth, and the smell of Pine Sol. He tried to move but found himself restrained and tied to his dining room chair with a phone cord. He looked to his right and saw his beautiful wife limp and wrapped in a sheet and tied as he was in a phone cord to a dinette chair.

"Meggin, Meggin honey!" he yelled out, but got no answer.

"Nigga, shut yo ass up, she gone be alright."

He turned to see his uncle scrubbing the floor and everywhere he touched. "Unc, what's going on? What's this about? Why you doing this to me?" Dubb asked hysterically, frightened.

"We gon get to the bottom of that. Just wait a minute." Ben-K finished what he was doing and came and sat in front of the couple. Dubb was so scared, he pissed on himself. He wasn't even worried about his wife no more. All he cared about was his own safety.

"What chu gon do to me, Unc?"

Ben-K shushed him with his finger to his lips and spoke calmly. "Nephew, you disappointed me."

"But I—" Dubb tried to speak but Ben-K shushed him again and finished.

"Nephew, you let niggas kill my boy, and then you turn around and make peace with these same dudes who did it? It's niggas like you who put a black eye in the game fo real."

Ben spoke and Dubb listened. He didn't want to frustrate Ben no more than he was now. He knew he was already on borrowed time anyway. All he could do was sit there and drop tears.

"Tell me everything and which one pulled the trigger. Then give me all the cream and all the money you got. I even want the cars and jewelry too. Yo ass don't deserve none of that shit, plus that's yo ticket to live with that pretty wife of yours," Ben stated.

After hearing that, Dubb knew he would live. He started to protest, but Ben continued. Ben saw the reluctance in Dubb's eyes and quoted, "It's harder for a rich man to make it into Heaven than it is for a camel to make it into the eye of a needle. So just consider yourself blessed."

Ben sat back as Dubb explained to him the whole story and where to get all the money and merchandise. About the time he finished, Meggin came to and was about to scream again, but her mouth was gagged with a scarf. Her good one too. She looked at her helpless husband and cried as her protector sat crying as well. This was not the provider she loved all these three years of marriage. This was not the strong man she never saw shed a tear before. Her thought of him took on a whole new meaning. She told herself after this was over, if she survived, she was leaving his weak black ass for sure. The calm strength that Ben-K displayed, for some strange, sick reason, gave her pussy a tingle. She didn't know that this was Dubb's uncle. But her tears subsided and her legs gaped open, revealing her golden nature. Ben-K ignored her advance and kept talking.

"Nigga, Ima let you live, but I want you and this white piece of trash out of town and never come back. Only reason you living is because of my sister, but if I ever see or hear of your ass back around town, I'm not gon give a fuck, ya dig?"

He looked in Dubb's eye and then at Meggin. The urge to kill at least her ass ran through his mind, but the instinct she gave him assured him she wouldn't call the cops. After gathering up all the money, jewelry, and dope, and jotting down the address to the other spot, Ben took the car keys, cut them loose, and left out the door.

CHAPTER 15

Little Vick stood in the line at Macy's inside Bay Fair Shopping Mall in San Leandro. His hands were so full of bags of Sean Jean outfits he couldn't even answer his cell phone. The way he felt, he probably would have ignored it anyway. Last night he had a fallout with KP over some bullshit-ass dope fiend who owed KP. But Vick served him before KP could demand his money from the knock. KP beat the knock ass and Vick protected him. He and KP almost squabbled if Noonie hadn't broken it up. Vick had already told KP not to be beating on knock before. And that the same knocks are the same ones you see when you go to jail. They be swoll up and shot callers in the BGF. But that didn't scare KP because he always shot back that his dad was a shot caller in that same gang. He and Vick had their words and that was that. But Vick was still pissed off about that.

He surveyed that store of patrons and cracked a smile at this midget dressed in all green. His big-ass head was what caught Vick's attention. He overlooked him and noticed another bald-head dude mean muggin. He overlooked dude too and paid for his clothes. He pulled out a thick bankroll, paid the cashier, picked up his bag, and left out the store. He was strolling and didn't have a concern as he left the mall. He made it to his car and sat the bags on the ground by the trunk. He reached in his pocket for his keys and heard, "Nigga, don't move! Move over there."

The gunman motioned with the pistol for Vick to move to the side of his car in between this van and his car. Vick did so without question or a word. He was mad, though, because he got caught slipping and he didn't have a pistol in his waistband. This one time he decided to leave it under his car seat. He did smirk as he thought those thoughts. Through his glass side mirror he could see that same bald-head he saw in the store. *Damn, I knew that nigga didn't look right,* he thought. *But who is this dude and why he got something against me?* Vick was baffled.

Dude was only about three inches shorter than Vick but he was a good 20 pounds heavier. He snatched the car keys out of Vick's hands and kept the gun trained on Vick's head. He drew back and went to slap Vick upside the back of his head and Vick decided differently. Vick slung his dreds around, making them slap dude in the eye. Reflex made dude squeeze the trigger. *POW!* The gun went off. Vick turned around, grabbing dude's wrist with the gun in hand while connecting his fist with dude's chin. Vick pressed dude against the van and the impact made dude release the gun. Vick kneed dude in the nuts, making dude bend over in pain. Vick combined punches to dude's face swiftly. Dude dropped to the ground and Vick started stomping dude ferociously.

All the while, more people came out, witnessing the brutal beating. Vick was so into the ass-whopping that he didn't even see the mall security approaching until they tackled him. Vick was so irate, he even kicked one guard. They held Vick until the real police came and secured the scene, taking Vick to jail for assault and taking dude to the hospital. They never found the gun because it slid under a car. Luckily for Vick, they didn't; they were even nice enough to let Vick grab his keys off the ground and lock his bags in his car. By Vick not being on probation, they couldn't search his car. He told the police that he and dude were fighting over a girl they both messed around with. And since dude didn't press any charges, Vick was released three days later.

Shawnie sat in the driver's seat of Vick's car, demolishing a pickle with a peppermint stick sticking out of it. This was her third one already that day. The whole inside of her mouth was red. She knew something was wrong because she never even liked pickles growing up. Now all of a sudden her insides craved them. Her menstrual was seven days late and it still hadn't come yet.

Vick sat in the passenger seat wondering why she hadn't driven off yet. Sitting in front of this police station was making him nervous all over again. Shit, he barely escaped a prison term, and those three little days felt like three years in there.

"Shawnie!" Vick snapped. "What chu waitin on? Get me the fuck outta here, fore them people find some mo shit to keep my black ass up in there."

Shawnie started the car and pulled off. She drove down Broadway in silence, eating her pickle. She noticed out of the corner of her eye Vick was watching her. She broke the silence.

"Hey, baby! I'm sho glad you outta there. I missed you so much. I been at home waiting for you. It seemed like a year. Baby, I love you an all, and I'll always be there for you, but baby, this jail shit ain't cool, especially with me being pregnant." She stopped talking, realizing what she said for the first time in her life.

It took only a second for Vick to catch on, but when he did: "You what?!" His expression was fierce. He made her think he was. "What the fuck you mean, pregnant? I ain't ready for no kids! Plus how you know it's mine?"

That changed Shawnie's whole coolness. She expected Vick to be a little upset, but never did she think he would deny her sureness. Her temper flew through the roof of the car. She made a right on MacArthur and headed to the freeway entrance. She smashed the gas pedal. The car leaped to 80 miles per hour, and she cried while cursing Vick out with every curse word known to man and even some unknown.

"Mutha fucka, how in the fuck you gon question that shit? You think I'm one a them other bitches, what? You think I'm a hoe or something? Fuck you, mutha fucka, I don't need you, I can raise my baby all by myself!" she spat, tears flowing down her face like a river. She was pissed off beyond measure. She smashed the gas pedal as the car passed and weaved through the thick traffic. She drove like a madwoman. She drove like a drunken madwoman. Barely missing a SUV, Shawnie was deliberately trying to show Vick that she didn't give a fuck.

Vick was spooked at the ranting and raving that Shawnie had going on. "Shawnie, calm down, stop actin stupid before you kill us!" Vick shouted. The car swerved again, this time scraping up against the guardrail.

"So I'm stupid too?!" Shawnie shot back.

Vick was scared and nervous reflexes made him grab the steering wheel. Shawnie's foot slammed the brakes. Vick was able to guide the car into the emergency lane safely while forcing the car in park and snatching the keys out of the ignition at the same time. Shawnie snatched her seat belt off, jumped out of the car, and started walking down the side of the freeway, pissed off. At first Vick was going to just let her keep walking, especially after she almost killed both of them in her angry fit of reckless driving. But it was that fire in her that he loved about her. She was not no punk bitch scared to face him. He smiled at the crazy thought of her and gave chase.

When he caught up to her a quarter mile away, he spun her around to face the tears she mirrored. Vick being in love with her made it easy to consider her emotions and sympathize with the situation. She looked so good standing there with those red lips. He smiled at her and that was all it took to melt her cold heart. He embraced her while speeding traffic blew by, blowing their horns at the kissing lovebirds.

CHAPTER 16

L oud Mexican music filled the air and Marlboro smoke suffocated the room. Corona bottles and shot glasses filled with Patron and tequila littered the tables. Cowboy hats, tight shirts, tight jeans, and cowboy boots were scattered around; some playing pool, some at the bar, some at the gambling tables, and some just looking on. Spanish chicks clung to their honchos and chicos held their chicas. You could see who the big shots in the rooms were because while they played the games, their bodyguards stood their positions, observing the scenery. The lingo was all Spanish and not one other race of people was in the room. The atmosphere represented Mexico to the fullest. It was around the time of the national soccer championship and all the TV screens around the room were on ESPN/Spanish channel.

One guy sat at the bar dressed like a modest regular: faded jeans and jacket, boots and cowboy hat. One guy sat at his right, one at his left. While he drank his Corona, they just sat and watched. All eyes turned to the door's entrance as a man in jeans, a white tee, and a baseball hat stood there. The music kept going but the conversations stopped immediately, until the guy at the bar looked up and spoke. "El cachazudo, amigo!" (He's cool, friend.)

Pablo Sanchez gestured to Jason to come sit with him at the bar. Just as fast as the conversation stopped, that's just how fast it started back up. Everybody in there knew that Pablo owned the building. And they also knew that he dealt with a lot of black folks. So if he said it was cool, then it was cool. He whispered something in Spanish to the two guys next to him, and they got up and went to the other side of the bar. Jason ordered a cranberry double.

"Que paso, amigo?" Jason asked.

"Not much, my friend, how are you?" Pablo asked.

"I'm good, just been chillin, tryin to line things up in the hood, that's all. I'm glad you could meet with me," Jason stated.

"No problem, my friend. All things that are good come together for the good purpose. I would have eventually came to you or Rick sooner or later. I thought it may have been Rick more likely. He seems the more quieter, you know, my type." He paused, took a sip of his Corona, and asked Jason, "So, how much do you need to run your operation?"

Jason was thrown back by Pablo's straightforwardness, but he liked it more so. Jason wasn't good at negotiating, but he knew the basics. He knew what the prices were going for and he knew what he needed.

"Wow, Papi, straight to the point, huh? That's cool. I need about at least fifty a month to do what I need to do."

Pablo let out a husky but mocking gesture. "Ha, is that it? I thought you guys were moving at least a hundred. I guess that shows me, huh? Can't always tell a book by its cover. Well, my friend, I only move loads by the hundred pack. For me to move fifty would be for me going backwards, amigo, and that I don't do. But I tell you what, I'll do it for you, seeing that you have cahoonas, and I like that. I'm gonna make you richer than you've ever imagined. I never be empty and I always keep the best. I'll have one of my men deal with you guys. This will be the last time you and I will meet, comprende?" He didn't wait for an answer. "For security reasons, you pay for your fifty and I'll put up the other fifty for you. Same time every month. All of that only on one condition." He paused for that to sink in Jason's head.

Jason wondered on what condition this would be. On what terms. How many hoops he had to jump through. This was the connect he and Rick had been looking for all their young lives in the game. And Jason knew in his heart that he would do anything to lock this line in. Jason looked up at Pablo and asked, "What?"

"Simply," Pablo looked Jason dead on in his eyes very seriously and continued, "stop fucking my wife."

At first Jason was drained of all the man in him. Fear set in and then his eyes revealed surprise. He looked around the room and saw a sea of Mexicans. He thought of running out the door, guns blazing, at first. But then he settled and realized that if he wanted him dead, all that conversation would not have happened. Pablo noticed his nervousness.

"Don't worry, my friend. I knew she was a fuckin' slut whore way back when. You're not the first. The whore slut so fucking stupid, she doesn't realize she's sleeping with the enemy. Her best friend and I been fucking for five years now, and she tells me everything the whore tells her. She's only enjoying the fruits of my labor because of my kids. Little Pablo wanted to kill her himself. He told me also what you guys did to him and he had me swear not to order your deaths. It is him who told me of your loyalty in your organization. He gave me the whole layout."

Jason listened intently, relieved and anxious. Turns out that little Pap was more real than he'd thought. He had Jay's and Rick's lives in his hands and instead of having them whacked unsuspectingly, he plugged them right in. Jason was so grateful he didn't hear the last part.

"Huh?"

"I said, that is the reason why I want you to stop fucking my wife. To show me loyalty. To be a part of my family, it takes loyalty. And family don't fuck family in no types of shape, form, or fashion."

He watched Jason in both eyes. Jason didn't have to even think twice. He knew he cared about her but not enough to get killed for her. After Jason's assured nod, Pablo continued.

"You know, Jason, my Mexican mafia is stronger than any cartel around the world. I've ordered more deaths over disloyalty than for money owed to me. That's something I don't tolerate. So I will leave you with this warning. Never try to fuck me, Jason. It's not about where you from or what you done. It's about where you are at and how you act that matters."

He held a cold, sweaty stare at Jason to the point where tears almost filled his eyes. For the first time in life, Jason felt scared.

He slammed the door to his car, where Rell sat holding a mini 14 assault rifle. Rell's little baby face could see by the look on Jason's face that he was bothered. But he didn't say anything, he just sat ready for a command to go up in that mutha fucka and make enchiladas out they ass.

*　　*　　*

Back on the block, loud gunfire erupted out the window of an Astro van. No one could make out the faces due to the black ski masks that covered them. Only thing they saw was fire coming from the barrel of about ten guns. When the van first turned the corner, Noonie was suspicious of it. He was the only one who paid attention. Even the lookouts on the rooftop didn't pay it no mind. About time it got to the crowd, it was too late. Unexpectedly, three dope fiends got hit from the barrage of bullets. Noonie let off all the 30 rounds he held inside of the Mack 11 he was holding. The van cruised by slow enough to make sure that they hit somebody. No particular person outside at the time mattered. The primary target wasn't in sight. But someone had to get it good. It sounded like World War III out there. It seemed that the gun sounds from the van wouldn't stop. The lookouts on the roof were both so stunned, their fingers squeezed their triggers, but their aims were useless.

All 30 of Noonie's bullets hit the van's exterior, rattling it, but there was no effect to the shooters. Noonie tried his hardest to push his overweight body over the fence of a neighbor's yard, but he just couldn't manage it. *POP, POP, POP, POP, POP!* Sounds came toward him; he went to turn and run but was met by more shots. *POP, POP, POP, POP!* As big as a target Noonie was, only one bullet out of all nine shots fired hit him. But that one was the one that ended his life. The bulled hit him in the center of the forehead directly in his skull, opening up the back of his head when the bullet flew out. Noonie's body dropped to the ground with a slam. He punched the ground with one fist as if to say, "Damn! I got caught out of pocket. Them niggas got lucky." Then his body lay there leaking all of his body's blood life out of it and the concrete ate it up.

The shooters in the van sped off after all of their horrific damage was done. The scene they left was a disaster field. Broken windows, bullet-riddled cars, house paneling holey, bodies laid out, screams and cries, broken lives and confused minds. All of the occupants of the van wore smiles under their ski masks except one: the driver. Ben-K was disappointed that the killer of his nephew was not out there. Personally, he didn't want anyone to pay for the responsibility of one man's wrongdoing. But what can you tell a bunch of young trigger-happy niggas, he thought. Nothing! Even all the young niggas in the crew couldn't amount to half the nigga he was. They trying to get there, though. And he was trying to stop. *The cycle keeps going around and around*, he thought. He then drove the van to their designated place and torched it.

About the time they switched cars and made it to their safe house, Ben-K was tired, mentally and physically. All the energy the young boys exuberated around him had sucked out all the little bit he did have. Being around all these younger dudes wasn't too bad as company was concerned, but these little niggas were just too damn hyper for an old man like K. He realized to himself that it was time for him to be retired. He looked around the room at all the young dudes smoking and drinking, playing dominos, eating pizza, talking on their phones, and chilling. They all revered Ben-K. They looked up to him like he was God. There weren't too many O-G's in the game that got that kind of respect from youngstas. He smiled at that thought.

One of his young homies saw him in thought, and walked up and disturbed his groove. This youngsta had that aura that K liked himself. He was relaxed and easygoing but serious and a head-buster. And K liked that. He didn't have dreds like the rest. He worked a Caesar cut, no gold teeth, and he didn't drink or smoke. He dressed nice and kept a clean cut. His fair skin and his brown eyes won him all the young girls. His pigeon-toed stride glided up to K.

"What's up, old man." He smiled.

Ben-K looked up at the smile he liked and an instant smile surfaced on his face. "Hey, young T, what it be, little homie? You been practicing your aim, I see," Ben-K smiled devilishly.

Young T smiled back. "What chu over here thinking about? You alright? I know what it is already, but don't trip though. We gone get that nigga, Unc. That's on everything."

They chopped it up about all the things on Ben-K's mind. They talked all the way until the next day. They planned on going through that hood until they caught little Vick outta pocket and killed him. It was on and it was that serious. Ben-K looked up at young T and smiled as he thought, *It's youngstas like you that made the reason and turned the thoughts I had when I was released from prison: to come home and kill all them hyper dumb-ass little niggas who fucked off the game.*

CHAPTER 17

The yard was thick and full of inmates. A large blue sea of some of the world's most hardened criminals walked the track in two's. Some worked out on the bars while others watched their backs. Whites with whites, blacks with blacks, and Mexicans with Mexicans. Indians sweated in their section under the teepee. Usso's and others did their own thing in their place. The sun baked and beamed down hard on the open space, as did all the prison CO's. One in the gun tower eyed each prisoner through his high-powered lensed telescope on top of his mini 14 assault rifle. At the card tables an African tribe called Kumi surrounded their leader in a meeting. Most of them were younger dudes with a few elders in the group. Another table had four seats with four older men playing a game of pinnacle, the jailhouse's most famous card game. These men were more laid back from growing old on the yard together all those years. They were the four heads of the world's oldest black penitentiary gang, the BGF. Groups of black serious stone-faced men held oose (protection) around them.

Today was a good day so far. The yard was just relaxed off lockdown. They'd been locked down for about six months due to a riot which left 14 stabbed and two deaths. The southern Mexicans against the northern ones. The majority had been sent to the hole. And the ones on the yard now were not functioning ones.

An older, smooth-faced gentleman with a silver head of waves smiled to his penitentiary bombshell, the closest thing you can get to a woman in prison, approaching. His muscular frame turned slightly and he leaned his ear close. Sheila, born Paul Stental, whispered something in his ear. Kersy Patrick's smile faded at the news of his boy getting shot. He may not have been there for his twin boys financially or physically, but this was one term of endearment he'd been waiting to show all these years. After delivering the message, Sheila sashayed away gracefully.

All the other gorillas knew something was up immediately. Killa P smiled a lot and he rarely showed the murderous eyes of his. His four life sentences still hadn't changed his killer affection he displayed. He got to the point to where now all he had to do was send the word. And once his word went forth, it was valid like a god. He had lieutenants and soldiers all over the United States, and all of them were loyal to their code of ethics. The unspoken word was sent from across the card table with a nod and it went forth from there to so on. And just like that, a hit clan was signaled right from inside the prison from the card table. Killa P resumed his card game as if nothing was ever said. Back smiling, knowing that his order would be done.

CHAPTER 18

After talking to Jason, Rick headed to the spot to check on the crew of amp youngstas. When he got there, the whole hood was taped off with yellow police barrier tape. He drove right past. From there he drove to the hospital where Ray Ray was being held. After Ray Ray finished being interrogated and telling the police he didn't know who or why he got shot, they left. Ray Ray's legs were in severe pain; he could even feel the pain up in his chest. It was bad. Rick walked in and sat beside him on the chair. He loved the twins as his own sons, so hearing one of them was lying up dead from an assault on their life hurt him pretty bad. KP and the other youngstas were out there in the traffic riding around, terrorizing anyone who even looked suspicious. They felt that this was a good opportunity to go lay the law down on everybody who fell out their radar.

Vick was so mad he wasn't even talking. He just let his SK assault rifle talk for him. The town just didn't know what it all was for. And Ben-K just didn't know the drama he and his crew had started. These little dudes were young, but they were cold-blooded killers. No mercy.

Rick knew that there was nothing that could be said to tame his crew. And plus, his ethics of the game knew he had no choice but to let it all flow. But he, being smart about it, just wanted to know who was behind it, and then he could kill the head of the problem. Rick studied all the arts of war, the 48 laws of power, the rules of combat, and many other books of war. He knew that if you kill the head and maybe a few other followers, the rest would fold.

"How you feel, little bruh?" Rick asked with a smile, trying to bring some cheer.

"I'm good, bruh. This shit just hurt like hell, though, but I'll live. I'm cool, though. Them bitch-ass niggas caught us slippin. They got some of our most faithful customers, but luckily they ain't get no soldiers. Well, except Noonie." Ray Ray teared at the wound and patches on his leg. The doctors just needed to run a few more tests and they were going to let him go.

"You didn't get a chance to see who did it or who was shooting?" Rick asked.

"Naw, all them niggas was wearing masks, plus it was dark and hella crowded outside. That nigga Bill said he saw some niggas around the corner putting on masks, though, inside a van, but he couldn't get around to tell us about it in time, though. He said one of 'em looked familiar, the driver—said he looked like this old-school nigga named Ben-K."

That name hit Rick quick right off the bat. He heard a lot about the dude but never met him. But he did know that he was related to ol' boy and his cousin. Rick thought, *I knew that nigga Dubb was gon double-cross us!* All Rick could think about now was how much he couldn't wait to kill that nigga. They waited around until the doctor cleared Ray Ray and they left.

Rick and Ray Ray met Jason, Vick, and KP at the Big O Tire Station on 98th and International Boulevard. Jason ran over a nail in the street and he had a slow leak in his tire. The sun was baking hot and warm. Traffic was moderate and McDonald's was packed. All the out-of-school kids filled the place. Across the street, the AMPM Mini Mart was also packed. Jason sent Vick to the Kentucky Fried Chicken two buildings over to get them a bucket of chicken. He thought it was better to eat fried chicken instead of eat McDonald's.

About a year ago, Jason had a near-death experience with a McDonald's drive-thru. Not with the food either. He was sitting in his car with a new honey he met. He thought he knew her well enough to let her use his car one day prior. Apparently she, being unaware of the dudes tailing her three cars behind, had led them right back to the hotel she and Jason were staying in. The dudes knew Jason's car and they waited on them to come out. And that took all the way until the next morning's check-out time. They were going to take them then but too many witnesses were out. They had a grudge to settle with Jason over an old weight issue about some prices. They followed them to

McDonald's because Jason wasn't about to spend another dime more on this chick. He told himself that day he wished he hadn't been so cheap. While he waited, the passenger approached his side of the car. From a distance the perpetrator started shooting out of fear. Jason didn't move but the girl started screaming and hollering for her life. But luckily the shooter was a bad shoot, because neither Jason nor the girl was scratched with a bullet. Jason was strapped but didn't get a chance to get off one shot. The attempted murderer fled the scene with his driver and Jason calmly drove his bullet-hole-covered car out of the drive-thru and he vowed to never eat at another McDonald's again. And he had been sticking to his vow faithfully.

"You seen that nigga Dubb yet?" Rick asked.

"Naw, I'm waiting for him to call me so I could dump this shit on him. I ain't heard from that nigga since the last time I saw 'em. I been havin to bus other moves just to keep this shit moving. Luckily, it's some good shit and the prices is cool," Jay said.

Neither one of them knew that Dubb would not be coming back to California, ever. Dubb and his luggage took the plane all the way to Missouri. That's where he was able to buy him a nice little cottage for him and his wife. He thought she would be coming to join him after he got settled, but it had been six months now and he still hadn't heard nothing from her. Dubb found him a delivery job and had been doing good without selling even a crumb of dope. He often thought that he should have been living this way of life in the first place. If only he would have been thinking back then. Life would have been much easier.

"Remember when I told you that bitch-ass nigga was up to something?" Rick stated.

"Yeah, and fuck that nigga, we don't need his fuckin' money anyway. That nigga was hot as hell too, so fuck 'em. I've been sellin this shit hella fast still and I ain't seen them Feds back since either," Jason stated matter-of-factly. He smiled while little Vick walked up with a bucket of chicken.

Vick gave the bum sitting next to the corner of the building a couple pieces and turned back around with a piece in his mouth. He placed his gold grill inside the car and set the bucket on the trunk. Ray

Ray grabbed him a piece and demolished it. It had been a minute since he had some real food. That hospital food was too gross for him. Plus they only fed him through an IV. The ice cream was good, though. He grabbed two more pieces and chomped them down too.

"This chicken good den a mutha fucka, boy." He had grease and chicken debris all over his mouth.

"Yeah, that's cool," Rick continued. "But that's not what I'm talkin' bout. Bill told Ray Ray he seen that nigga uncle mask up right before the spot got shot up. And you already know how that nigga get down. His ass don't stop until it's a done deal. So I know already that his ass gon be back. This time, we gon be ready for his ass, though."

Those little 20 pieces of chicken didn't last any time between the four of them. And counting the two pieces the bum got helped the banishment even more.

"Ay, Vick man, you gon have to lay low for a minute, cause I know by now that dude know who smacked his nephew," Rick stated, looking at Vick with cautious eyes.

Vick, on the other hand, was thinking differently. "Man, fuck that nigga, I'll flatten that old-ass nigga. That nigga might got ya'll spooked, but not me. Fuck him and feed him fish!" Vick was hot. He couldn't believe his OG homies were telling him to lay low like he's some sucka or something. But Jay, noticing the young dumbness in his youngsta, had to set him straight.

"Hold on, little nigga, it ain't got nothing to do with being spooked. I tell ya'll young asses all the time a mind is a terrible thing to waste. It's about being smart. Some niggas kill for bread and meat. It's they job. And it's about choosing your enemies wisely. It's a certain way you have to go about knockin certain niggas down. And this nigga is one of them certain niggas. Now for you, nigga, the reason why we say lay low is because it's hard to hit a moving target. But it will frustrate his ass that he can't find you. And that will make his ass come to us. Then this time, we'll see his ass coming from a mile away, ya dig?"

When Jay finished his spiel, even Rick was impressed with how Jay's thinking and plan was so intelligent. When it landed in Vick's mind, he smiled and looked at Ray and KP smiling also. It was a good idea. Rick and Jay agreed to send Vick and KP and Ray to Atlanta to stay in their four-bedroom house they bought last year. And they got to take their little girlfriends if they could go. KP and Ray's little chicks were loose and they knew that theirs was locked in already, no question. It was Vick's girl that was going to have to convince her momma to believe she was going to go stay with some friends. It was already a heart-stopper on her momma when Shawnie told her she was pregnant and keeping it. And her momma was nobody's fool either. When Shawnie told her a lie to leave, she saw right through it. But still and all, she let her go eventually.

Juan, the tire service manager, came and let Jay know his car was ready and they all split up and left. Jay's plan came into effect that very day. They allowed Vick and Ray and KP to go pack and grab their girls. Their plane left at 11:30 p.m. that night, and Jay and Rick set up lookouts on each corner and even around the corners. They made sure every man on the block had a strap on them, servers or not. No man was strapless; each man with high-powered communication walkie-talkies. Never again would they slip.

CHAPTER 19

Erica sat in her apartment that Rick got for them. It was lavishly furnished throughout the entire house. It was in a gated community in the finer neighborhood of pleasant valley Dublin, California. Rick got fed up with the cost of the hotel rooms, and thought it was safe now since they hadn't heard any news of Erica being wanted for the murder of Mac. Rick figured everything was cool now. Erica's real name wasn't known to Mac's hoes and with Mac's demise, the hoes felt liberated anyway. Mac's bottom hoe, his wife, cleaned the safe out behind the refrigerator and skipped town. Erica's fed-up fear was an actual escape route for all who were under Mac's subjections. And by Mac's profession being considered by the locals as "the scum of the earth," they put the investigation on the back burner. Erica was a free woman—finally.

She leaned back on her peanut-butter leather relaxer chair, rubbing her stomach, smiling. Although sometimes she thought of the police kicking her door in and arresting her, she felt safe in Rick's care. She watched TV and continued to rub her stomach. She didn't rub it because of the half a pizza and bottle of Pepsi she guzzled down. Erica knew something else. Something familiar that she was accustomed to all too well. She was pregnant. She knew the symptoms very well; the nipple tenderness, the appetite, and the absence of her period confirmed it. The only one who didn't know was Rick. And she didn't know how to tell him either. She was worried at how he would take the news. She was in so much deep thought that she didn't even hear him come through the door.

He looked around at how beautifully Erica had decorated the apartment. He had been letting her go do all the shopping. He figured it would get her mind off all the drama she'd been through. And like most women, it did help her. He looked at the half pizza on the counter and smiled. After a stressful day of the streets, Rick always felt at ease when he came home to Erica. She was his heart's safe haven. He watched her over there and the jingle of his house keys landing on the counter startled her. *Ching!*

"Oooh!" She turned, half frightened, with one hand under the couch pillow holding the .25 automatic handgun Rick bought her.

"Baby, don't kill me, it's only me," Rick laughed. "I'm sorry daddy scared you."

He grabbed a slice of pizza as he eased up over to her. He sat on the arm of the chair and slid-snuggled under her. They kissed and he stuffed his face with pizza, talking with food in his mouth. "So, what my baby been doing today?"

She looked shocked, as if he already knew she was pregnant, eyes bugged, rubbing her stomach. "Nothing, Boo, just chillin' today. I need some girlfriends; being stuck in this house is killing me with loneliness."

He felt it coming on, another one of her boredom speeches. He knew she was right, though, but Rick didn't trust no hoes in the street. as many hoes he had that helped him set up other niggas in the street. Hell naw, Rick wasn't having it. He knew better than that.

"Naw, naw, Boo. You already know how them hoes can be. We got too much to lose to let a snake get in."

With that, she knew it was the right time to break the news.

"Well, I need something. What about a baby?" she asked in a whining tone, testing him.

"What about a dog?" he said half jokingly.

Her face puppy-dogged at the notion. He saw it and a smile formed on his face. "Just kidding, Boo, but are you ready for a baby this time? Your other two are fine, but they still need you. I wouldn't want my baby without its mother. I'd probably kill you myself," he said seriously.

That was his biggest fear about having children by women. He didn't want any broken homes. That had been one of his pet peeves since his dad left him. He vowed that his kids wouldn't ever be without their mom or dad.

"Yes, I'm ready," she said as the tears welled up in her eyes. "It's nothing more that I want more than to have my own family with you. And that way I can prove to the courts and my momma that I'm ready to be a loving mother to my kids."

He saw how sincere she was and it made him feel good and proud for her to be finally stepping up and moving past the obstacles in her life. Her crying started getting more hysterical. He grabbed her in his arms.

"Shhh, shhh, shhh, calm down, baby, calm down. You know I love you too. And a baby would be perfect to go with this."

Rick reached in his pocket and pulled out a box small enough for a ring. He handed it to her. She nervously accepted it. Tears of sadness instantly turned to tears of joy. She opened the box and a 10-karat platinum engagement ring sat there. Rick couldn't even get the question out.

"Yes, yes, yes, I do!" Erica screamed, jumping all over him, kissing him all over his face. She was so happy. Happier than she'd ever been in her life. She slipped the ring on herself and admired how beautiful it looked.

Rick had gone and cashed out at the jeweler earlier that day. He paid 15 racks. He got a deal because he did so much business there. But it didn't matter. Rick didn't care about the price to make his Erica happy. He watched the glow of happiness on her face. She straddled him and felt his monster harden up. She leaned to his ear and nibbled softly. Then she whispered, "Big boy can take it easy, and he don't have to work hard tonight. I'm pregnant already, daddy."

She tried to back up to see his expression, but he pulled her into him. They kissed joyously and they passionately stripped each of their clothing and made love all over the apartment.

CHAPTER 20

Inside the abandoned house was murky, watery puddles, broken windows, and glass-covered areas of the floor. Syringes and old used condoms were scattered around too. One could see that this was a dope fiends' shop and prostitutes' place. Any person who walked in, if they weren't cops, already knew what time it was. Handle your business and keep it moving. Some nights, it would be slow like a graveyard. And some nights, it looked just as that. So many bodies would be lying around doped up and stinking. It would stink so bad that sometimes people would swear that there were dead bodies in there.

Sherilyn, Rob, Lenny, crooked-eyed Dave, and Ronda Pearl just copped from the crew around the corner. They stepped into the infested smoke palace. They didn't even think of sharing their fix with nobody but themselves and that's it. Between the five of them, that one gram was not nearly enough, but at $25 a gram, they were going to make damn sure they got their share.

It had been some days since the five of them had been to the shack to do their business. They had been using Lenny's place to shoot up while his wife was away attending a church convention down south. She had been praying for Lenny's recovery for years now. But she still kept the faith because she knew her God can perform the impossible and the unthinkable of miracles. And that's what it was going to take for old Lenny to be rescued. Only God could do it. Since his wife had been back in town, the crew was forced back to their home away from home. They had discovered a place inside the house that had never been used by anyone but themselves. They had come across it three months ago. And every time they weren't using it, they'd padlock it up.

They rushed through the living room past all the other fiends unnoticed. They went through the kitchen, down the stairs, and straight to the basement. The stinking smell they smelled upstairs got stronger as they reached the door to the basement. They notice that the padlock was off and the door was ajar. First thing crooked eyed Dave thought and said was, "One a them mutha fuckas den found our spot and using it." He was the bigger one out the crew. And he couldn't wait to get there and catch whoever it was in there. He was going to commence to put a vicious ass-whooping on their ass. He rushed through the door and covered his nose from the smell.

The others followed suit and froze in their tracks when Dave stumbled over and fell to the floor. Rhonda hit the light and Sherilyn let out a piercing scream.

"Aaaahhh!"

Lenny vomited his lunch all over the floor. Rob did the same. Dave stood up, covered in blood, disgusted. The scene was horrific. It looked like a bloodbath in there. Five bodies were laid out, stripped naked, with their privates in their mouths and throats slashed. Apparently four days ago, ten big, black, buff men stormed the crew around the corner. The crew of Dubb's boys who Ben-K was in charge of now. The ten dudes pulled up in work vans and jumped out with assault rifles. They caught the dudes that were in the van with K when they shot up the block of Noonie. The dudes were off guard out there, getting high off weed and sipping syrup. The ten dudes were BGF, apparently sent by Noonie's dad. However, their primary target was not in sight. But the others were. Since mainly a lot of BGF dudes use heroin, it was easy for them to find them.

Back inside the basement, it didn't take Sherilyn two seconds to whip out her cell phone and dial 911, and about the same time for the rest of them to barrel the hell out of there. Little did she know that she would have a shitload of interrogative questions to answer. And she also would be burning the smoke spot down too. Staying above water was over. Two boats would sink. And the old saying never failed: loose lips sank ships.

CHAPTER 21

Months later

Rick and Erica had been riding around all day. They were exhausted from all the walking around, shopping for the expected new addition. Rick especially was fatigued. But he loved the look on Erica's face when she smiled; seeing her happy was most joyous to Rick. Her being pregnant brought out the natural beauty she possessed even more. Her skin shone from its fullness. She illuminated every store she stepped foot in. Her belly protruded slightly for 4½ months of pregnancy. When they were in the Baby Gap all the other mothers gave her compliments and congrats. Their baby had to have all the latest clothing and baby accessories any baby could ever dream of. Rick intended to spoil this baby, especially by it being his first. Neither he nor Erica knew what "it" was yet, so they bought both boy and girl everything. Rick prided himself for being rich, and having the woman he loved and for being an expectant father. He felt flabbergasted with his place in life. Erica purchased him-and-her Cartier watches while shopping. He glanced at his and smiled at the time.

At one moment, Rick's world changed almost instantaneously. His car was filled with so many shopping bags, his view was obscured. He wouldn't see the Ford Mustang tailing him. His erroneous decision to put the bags in the back seat would turn out to be very costly.

Rick made an acute right turn onto his residential neighborhood street. Before abating acceleration, he noticed the front end of the Ford Mustang two car lengths behind him as he turned. Sticking to his accustomed routine, he circled his block twice, pretending to be lost. Reaching under the seat, he grabbed his 17-shot Glock 9 mm. He slowed down a bit and alerted Erica about what was about to go down.

She reached into her Gucci bag and grabbed her personal .25-caliber handgun with the pearl handle. She never went anywhere without it. She always feared a day like this would come. And lo and behold, here it was. Rick feared for his baby and Erica being in the midst of such an episode. But he refused to let his machismo be anything other than the real man he claimed to be. He and Erica had practiced occasionally for times like this. She already knew what to do.

Rick led the Mustang to a parked van and hopped out blazing. *Pop, pop, pop, pop!* His gun went off. The two thugs inside the Mustang must have been amateurs. The driver's foot smashed the gas and rammed into the back of Rick's car. He shot back at Rick and hit Rick in the arm, making Rick drop his weapon. The passenger of the Mustang stepped out with his gun blazing at Rick also. Rick fell on the side of the van near his weapon. He looked under the van and he could see the feet and legs of his assailants. Rick grabbed his gun and to his surprise, both feet didn't come toward him like he planned. One pair came toward him, and the other pair veered toward Erica. Rick's heart dropped in his pants. All he heard was the sounds of a small-caliber gun and four shots from a larger one. Rick shot at the feet and legs coming toward him and the guy fell to the pavement. Rick continued shooting, hitting the guy in the face and chest, killing him instantly.

Rick's heart jumped up out his chest faster than his body leaped from the ground. Rick's whole world became an aberration. It seemed that every second was five minutes apiece. Thoughts of Erica slumped over, bleeding from the head, cinematized Rick's mind. He made it to his feet, his shoulder leaking pints of blood.

He rounded the van cautiously, sticking his gun out ahead of him. He knew by now his gun was close to empty. His nerves had tears and agony, pain and anguish seeping through his sweat-drenched face. He made it to the side of his passenger side door. He saw the hit man laid out on his back, gasping and gurgling a mouth full of blood. His gun lay beside him while his hand held the hole in his neck. Rick put him out of his misery with a single shot to his ski mask. *Pow!*

He turned to find a bleeding Erica unconscious. "No, no, noooo!" Rick yelled out. He dropped his gun as he rushed to Erica's side. By now, neighbors came out and traffic had stopped to help. Rick checked her vital signs and he felt a pulse.

"Somebody call an ambulance!" he yelled. "Come on, E, hang in there, baby. You gon be okay."

Rick was crying heavily now and rubbing on Erica's face and rubbing her stomach. He heard sirens and tires screeching. Soon police arrived, drawing guns and securing the crowd. The paramedics got there and rushed out with the stretchers. They pulled Rick off of Erica and the police handcuffed him to a stretcher. He noticed the paramedic administering CPR to Erica. The assistants were checking the other two guys and the police were questioning Rick while he was being placed in the ambulance. His ambulance pulled off, leaving his mind full of paranoid despair as he watched from a distance.

CHAPTER 22

In any business or any type of corporation or organization, it is always the head or CEO or president or the thinker, the one who orchestrates, the organizer, who draws all the attention. He's the one who gets the most time in jail if his crew is busted. And when he and his crew step out to party or frequent some event, it's he who centers the attention. You know, "the man." Whatcha call 'em and them. Being a ghetto celebrity, word travels fast. Everybody who was somebody, and knew somebody who knew somebody, knew Rick had been shot. For only being in the hospital for just three hours, the whole of Oakland knew. Barber shops and hair salons gossiped. Every street-corner hustler spoke word of it.

Jay, KP, and Vick rode around town indiscreetly in a rented Lincoln Town Car. KP's mind was going crazy since his brother got killed. He was already a beast, but now he turned into a monster. At the funeral, he just sat there staring at the face of his brother lying in the casket. He never dropped not one tear. After they laid his brother to rest, that night, he went out all by himself through Dubb's spot and killed two people. And every night since, he had been killing somebody. And now it didn't matter who the victim was. He was not listening to no type of reasoning, or any excuses. He vowed to kill somebody every single night. And now that Rick had been shot, he was more than willing to kill. Some people don't like to funk; killing people is not for everybody. KP was not one of them. In fact, all three in the car were killing machines. They all loved it. So finding and killing the head of this problem was no problem.

They wouldn't go visit Rick because the police had him under arrest for the murders of those two hit men. He was undergoing surgery on his shoulder and right after that, he was being booked in the county jail. The only one who could visit him was his attorney right now. The doctor told him that Erica took a shot to the head and one to the shoulder. But surprisingly, she was still living. She was still unconscious and in a coma. She lost a lot of blood, but the baby was still alive too. She was in critical condition and undergoing brain surgery at this moment. That was good news to Rick, but at the same time bad news too. The doctor said if she pulled through, she'd most likely be a vegetable. Right now, it was not certain, and Rick's main concern was that she and the baby were alive.

Jason, Vick, and KP rode in silence. No radio or noise. The only sounds were the wind through the half-cracked window Vick had rolled down, and the evening noise of the ghetto streets of Oakland. It was a big difference from the Atlantic City weather. Vick missed his girl already. He and Shawnie did it up at the casinos, and made hours and hours of lovemaking. He smiled to himself at the thoughts of her crazy ass.

They were sitting at the stoplight on 73rd and International as they sat there committed to the thought of killing their archrival. A car behind them blew the horn, snapping them out of their still mode. *Honk, honk!* KP was seconds from opening the door and blasting the impatient driver. Jason sped off in the nick of time. The trio had been riding around all day together. Prior to Rick's altercation, they were checking traps and collecting money from debtors. They were headed to Bill's spot to just chill out and wait for a break as to where to find their elusive rival. Jason gave the whole hood the rest of the day off due to the day's incidents.

When they pulled up to Bill's house, they saw that the block was empty. They filed out with their hands on their weapons. Before they even made it to the door, Bill yanked the door open. He was holding the mini 14, wiping dried-up tears from his eyes, and grinding his teeth with an angry look on his face.

"Oh, it's y'all. I didn't know who the fuck it was pullin up to my house in that car. Y'all talk to Rick? How he doing, he gon be alright?" They couldn't even get inside the house fast enough before Bill had asked all those questions. Bill had been worried sick about Rick. He had to hear the news from a runner, and he was pissed about that too. Bill hadn't even gotten high since he heard the news.

They all came in the house and sat around the living room. Bill's house was old and it still had the same furniture he paid cash for back in the day when he first purchased the house. Every now and then, he would have one of his lady friends come over and clean up for him. The TV was on the news. It was talking about this situation.

"It's about time we finally got us somebody worthy to be a black president," Vick stated.

"Man, fuck Obama!" KP pessimistically spoke. "That nigga gon do just what them white folks tell 'em to do. They gon kill his black ass, watch."

"Nigga, stop hatin!" Jason defended. "We livin in history in the makin. Besides, if they kill that nigga, they gon start an all-out race war for real. See what I mean? When a nigga got his mind right, a nigga could fuck around and be president in this mutha fucka."

They smiled in agreement.

"I'm just sayin," KP spoke. "I sho hope that nigga can let my dad out of jail."

They got quiet and serious. Where that came from? They didn't know, but KP had never spoken of his dad before now. KP had never felt this much alone before either. He never was on this earth without his twin before. He needed somebody to fill that empty space.

"Why don't chu go see him then? He only forty-five minutes away and you all never went to visit," Bill said. Bill was sitting back a little ways off from the three. "You just don't know how much that would mean to him. Me being a father, all I do is wish and hope that my kids would come knocking on my door. I would even be happy to see they stankin-ass mama."

They all laughed. Bill finished talking after he ground his teeth.

"I don't know about that Osama, Olama, Otoma, or whatever the hell his name is. I just know as a people, we sho came a long ways from where I came from. It seem like just the other day Martin Luther King was having a dream. Now we got Obama fulfilling that dream. If we can just get the money without all this war shit, we'll be just fine. They need to let all those niggas in jail out. Send they ass over to Iraq and if they make it back, fuck it, they free. White niggas too. All they asses."

They laughed harder now. All the men felt at ease finally in each other's company. A few good laughs always soothe the troubled heart.

After the news, the World Series came on. They ordered pizza and sodas, and Bill went to the corner store and got some beer. KP went to the bathroom and came back out a totally different person. He just kept laughing and joking and clowning. Vick paid it no mind, but Jay thought it to be quite unusual. Vick rolled up two Philly blunts. He rolled them very fat too, like Jamaican style stick. He did that because it was Philly vs. the TB Rays. And his team was Philly.

"I got five hundred dollars on Philly," he stated.

"Bet!" KP hollered.

Bill came back in the house and handed Jay a piece of paper. "I seen little Pap's momma in the store and she gave me this to give to you. Man, that's a thick Mexican woman there. Ooh, wee!"

Ever since long ago, Jay stopped answering Mrs. Sanchez's phone calls. She would leave tons of messages on his voicemail, and she would leave notes on his car windshield. Jay's dick jumped from the thought of Mrs. Sanchez's good pussy. He was even tempted to break the code. But once he committed to anything, he maintained his loyalty. Plus her husband hadn't served him any bad dope yet to provoke him. He looked at the message.

> *My husband told me to give you this number: (213) 835-2111. He says some guy named Tyrone wants to talk to you or Rick. And call me, Papi, I love you and I miss your black dick very much.*

Jay sat back, cocked his head back to the side, looked at the note, and smiled. He thought to himself, old Pablo was testing him. He thought it to be amusing that the old man would try a move like that. Then Jay thought about the name on the note. "Tyrone," he mumbled to himself. Jay only knew one Tyrone.

Bill ground his teeth and walked up with a beer in his hand. "Jay, I didn't want to get her involved, but now this war has gone on too long with no solution."

Jay wondered what Bill was talking about. Bill continued, "Back in the days, this same nigga y'all getting into it wit used to terrorize back then the same way he do now. We all used to smoke together, me, him, a few of my ol' patnas, and his chick Silvia. When he went off to prison, me and Silvia would hook up and blow. Well, it became so often, that eventually we started fuckin."

Jay still wondered where the old man was going with this. "Man, who you talking about, who the fuck is Silvia?"

"The nigga killa's bitch. The nigga left that pussy out here and I was the nigga right there to scratch that itch." Bill spat triumphantly. "But stop asking questions and let me finish." Bill went on to tell Jay all about where Silvia lived and how they were going set up Ben-killa. While Jay listened to Bill, KP and Vick kept smoking purple haze and kicking back.

*　　*　　*

At the hospital, Rick sat back with an IV in his arm, his shoulder bandaged up with gauze, and hospital tape wrapped around his body. He felt like shit from all the dope he was shot up with. On top of that were the painful thoughts of his future wife and kid, and how they were doing. Rick thought about times of him thinking about getting out the game earlier, what business to open up. Diesel truck business named in honor of his deceased mother? Barbershop, landscaping, clothing store? He once considered real estate. Whatever his choice would have been, he beat himself up, wishing he had done it. The doctor told him Erica's condition was seriously stable and the baby was unharmed. She was still in a coma with no signs of coming out soon. The doctor planned to release Rick into the hands of the authorities once he was fully recovered, maybe in a week or two. His lawyer told him the case looked good for him due to the fact that the dead men had masks on and weapons were found on them. But Rick's only concern was about Erica and the baby.

CHAPTER 23

B en-killa sat quietly in a corner at a table inside Everett and Jones Barbeque on Broadway, downtown Oakland. All the customers and workers partied, celebrating victory on what should be considered the most extraordinary day in black history. Black America finally got the chance to serve one of its own: Barack Obama, the first African American President. Finally, black America got to see what all the past struggles of their ancestors were for. Marcus Garvey, Frederick Douglass, Rosa Parks, and Nat Turner, just to name a few; and the most profound two, Malcolm X and Martin Luther King Jr.'s prophetic "I Have a Dream" speech. Finally, the black race could see that hope was alive. All the black leaders of today could finally rest. The wall of perdition had finally come down between the races. The black race could finally feel accepted in America. And even some of the civil white folks in America could feel proud of their government, finally: Abraham Lincoln, John F. Kennedy, Bill Clinton, the first white/black president, and all those other Caucasians who tried and fought with black America side by side to make this country what it was today. Everyone in America could finally change the words to that old Negro folk song, "We Shall Overcome," to "We have finally overcome." There was not a sad face in the building. People screamed out, "Obama! Thank you, Jesus, praise God!" This was truly a day to be celebrated. When have you ever seen something like this? Never. If a person didn't believe in God, this was the time to start believing. Barack Obama represented a change. If he didn't change a single law while in office, his presence and his acceptance as President of the United States was worth a change for the people within itself.

Ben-killa had that very same thought on his mind as he sat there observing his surroundings. He himself had changed, a big difference.

Back in the prison, he led Bible studies. He always preached that change starts in a person's mind. In their way of thinking, to repent was to change. Barack Obama's entire campaign was based on change. Ben-killa stirred his coffee as he wondered the worth of all this murder he committed. His thoughts had two different outlooks. One thought: it was not for personal gain. Two, he thought, but it *is* personal. And in his mind, there was no other way to justify the situation. Somebody had to pay for his nephew's death. And not just anybody—the shooter. Ben-killa sat sipping his coffee and eating some of the best barbeque he'd ever tasted. He sat and planned his next strategic move on his opponent. He focused on the television and thought, *Change, huh? Well, I'm sho tryin. But these little niggas make it hard on an old nigga. Little stupid mutha fuckas.*

CHAPTER 24

Tamika sat on the corner of the inn table, panting. Her big yellow breasts rose and fell from deep breaths in and out her chest. Her extension braids were slung over her head wildly. Her entire body dripped profusely with her and KP's sweat. Yeah, KP's sweat. After the burial of his twin brother and her lover, she needed a shoulder to cry on and to help her get through the grieving stages of her loss. At first KP tried to do the best he could. But him looking identical to his brother didn't help. It did, but it didn't. It was like a Catch-22. And KP was caught right in the middle of it. It's not that he didn't love his brother or didn't respect him. He knew that was a line he knew not to cross. But at the same time, he felt that he was doing his brother a favor. He felt that it was his obligation to fulfill this space for his brother. And the Patron and blunts didn't change his judgment. Plus, all that powder KP had been snorting didn't help either. And the way Tamika's thick ass sat on her bodacious body was another enticement.

She watched KP as he washed up in the bathroom. She saw no difference between him and his deceased brother. In fact, they were exactly alike, even all the way down to their penis head. The only difference between them, she thought, was the way each one performed on her. Big difference, she thought; great big difference. And she loved it. Her little coochie was throbbing and pulsating from the way KP had put that dope dick on her. She knew she was in violation. But she had wanted a kid so bad with Noonie before he passed. All her friends were getting pregnant by their men and were happy. And then, poof! All her little dreams were vaporized when Noonie died. So, she thought, why not revive her fantasy with the next best thing, his twin brother?

She stood and walked inside the restroom to help KP finish cleansing himself. She grabbed the damp face towel out his hand and soaked it again with warm water. "Let me get that for you, big daddy," she said seductively. Her other hand rubbed his back while she kissed his dick head.

KP smiled and stood there, readily accepting his royal treatment. "Don't start this pile driver back up. You know yo pussy already in a recovery ward."

"How you figure I can't take no-mo?" she said in between slurps. With towel in hand, she slurped and slurped.

"Come on now, Meeka, I gotsta get ready fo I be late. That ride gon be at least two-three hours."

His dreds swung back and forth as he rocked from the way her mouth pulled on him. He wrapped his hand around the back of her head, entangling her extensions in between his fingers. "Ummpl!" he let out. *Slurp, slurp,* she bobbed.

Right when she knew he was ready to explode, she stopped and bent over the bathtub side. On her knees, she propped her ass up. She didn't want any of them juices to go to waste. KP, being not afraid of nothing, not even AIDS, and being very irresponsible, did not waste a second to get behind that big yellow ass. And it being perfectly round excited him even more. He gave her about ten good long, deep strokes before he let loose all his juices inside her. A quickie was all she'd get. He had places to go and people to see. She was glad he gave her pussy a break and had mercy on it. In fact, she just wanted that sperm anyway.

"Thank you, daddy. I needed that. Now I'll leave you alone so you could get dressed," she said as she marched to the bed.

"Why you won't come with me? That ride gon be real lonely," he said.

"Boo, if it ain't you in jail, I sho don't want to be standin in dem long-ass lines fo nuthin'. I'm sorry, babe, but I can't do it. Besides, you gon need that quality time alone anyway. I'll be right here waiting for you when you get back. You all kept me up all night anyway and I can use this time to get some sleep. Make sure you take the house key and you can drive my car too, I ain't goin nowhere today."

"Yeah, you right. I ain't seen this nigga since I was little. I might have to cuss this nigga out. Might even end up sockin this nigga in the mouth fa leaving and shit. I'm not even sho if I wanna even go see this nigga. I'm only doin this shit cuz my brother always wanted to go see this nigga. If it wasn't fa that, I wouldn't even do it. Fuck that nigga, far as I'm concerned."

KP started getting a little emotional as he spoke. He turned to shower and get dressed and prepare for this family reunion. Tamika understood exactly where he was coming from. Noonie had mentioned it to her a couple times about how he wanted to see his dad. She could relate because of her own dad's disappearing act he pulled on her mother. Fatigue overwhelmed her and she slipped into a deep sleep. She didn't even hear KP when he left out the door.

The ride all the way to Folsom State Penitentiary took a little under two hours, thanks to Tamika's '99 Nissan Maxima. KP thought it too funny that a dope dick would have a woman giving you keys to everything of hers. He diddy-bopped up to the gate. And after the long wait in line, the security search, and warrant checks, he was finally inside the visiting waiting area. He waited patiently while his dad and the other inmates who had visits were summoned in. From the looks of it, one would think that KP was in a regular state of mind. But inside his mind was a war. A war between love and hate. He loved his dad just because he was his dad. But he hated him for being absent in his upbringing. He and Noonie were too young to understand the reasons why their dad left them back then. And it was that young hate that KP held onto.

But as they themselves played the game, they came to realize the type of person their dad was: a soldier. And that made them love him for that. They heard stories about how their dad ran the streets with his gang and how he was an enforcer in the crew. He killed a lot of people for money and for just respect. And a lot of people feared him. He caught a life sentence for killing six guys for just disrespecting him in a club. He popped them right in front of everybody in the club. From the club, he got straight on a plane headed to Kentucky, didn't pack no clothes, tell his girl, his momma, nobody. He just left town. He stayed on the run for about five years before somebody saw his face on *America's Most Wanted*. Since then he'd been incarcerated and that was 20 years ago. Thanks to the streets talking, that was how KP and Noonie heard all the stories and whereabouts of their notorious dad.

And now, they'd finally get to be face to face.

CHAPTER 25

T he sliding door opened up for the inmates to proceed into the visiting room. They were all assigned to their own table. All the tables and chairs were small enough for preschool students to fit in. That's how whoever designed this setup wanted to make all the inmates feel, like they were all children. Grown men portraying life as young children playing. Playing with life, and themselves. Belittling one another's character. Killing one another, fighting and arguing over the smallest item or issue. Not being fathers and husbands to their families where it really counts. Lowering their mind state to the equality of a young kid. Grown men trapped in not only a prison behind the wall, but imprisonment of the mind. But that's exactly where the people who designed this system wanted the lost men to be. And to get out took knowledge, faith in God, and will power to do so. That was what KP's dad did daily. He read and studied law. And he also studied the law of the Bible, where the laws were derived from. For him to be such a mob figure and leader of a notorious gang, he was very smart.

He strolled in the visiting last. Still in good shape and in vibrant condition, he still had the glow of a youthful adult. Under his prison attire you could see that he worked out religiously. He scoped across the room of people with their families and friends. As he walked to his table, he spoke to some, slapped five with others. Everybody knew who he was. He stopped midway to his table and stood there. He saw an exact emulation of himself 30 years ago—32 years ago, to be exact. KP stood and looked on his earthly father in the same way. Except he saw a picture, a live picture of himself and how he would look 32 years from now, granted a good healthy lifestyle. Both men stood their ground like a young bull vs. old bull.

KP's dad made the first move in his continued stride toward his table. He walked straight up to his son and stood eye to eye. Neither one knew exactly what to do or what to say. Neither one really even knew each other. KP's dad thought back to his jail cell, where newspaper clippings hung on the wall with articles of his dead son. He stared at his son standing before him. He tried but he couldn't hold back the stream of tears that welled up in his eyes. He reached to grab and hug his son, but KP was rebellious in receiving him. His dad still held on to him while KP's arms hung to his sides. Then KP lashed out.

"Why? Why, man? Why!"

All the visitors and inmates stopped and looked on. The CO came charging over to their table. KP's dad just held on to his son tighter as both of their tears flowed.

"It's okay, son, it's okay, just let it out." He held up a hand to the rushing CO and the CO backed down and went back to his booth. A couple of inmates came to check on him and he assured them he was alright.

All that hard shit KP portrayed conceded. He was a little boy again. He always wanted to know why his dad wasn't around. All the street tales weren't enough answers for him. He still had emptiness in him. A whole lot of bottled-up tears, a whole lot of confusion now was able to be released. From one simple hug from his dad, KP calmed down and wrapped his arms around his dad. Both men stood hugging one another with tears of joy and pain streaming down their faces. Neither one willed to let go. Their embrace seemed to last a lifetime.

The CO flashed his flashlight on them, warning them to break it up. They did and they sat in the kindergarten chairs. His dad spoke.

"Damn, you look just like me." Silence, sniffles, and laughter. He continued, "I'm sorry, son. I wish…" Silence as he looked down in his lap. More tears fell.

KP spoke. "Don't worry about it." He paused. "Dad," he continued, "it was rough without you, but I understand. I guess when I saw you, I still had to let it out, but the streets raised me good. Me and my brother. And your reputation helped a lot too," he said with pride.

His dad sat with conviction of his son's words. He never wanted that type of life for his only two kids in life. But the cards were dealt and he had to play his hand, which was playing well until the death of his wife and their mother and his son Noonie.

"So, it looks like you turned out fine." He smiled "I always knew that Patrick's bloodline wasn't gon breed no punks anyway." They both shared a laughing smile.

"Naw, never that," KP spoke. "How you been holdin up in here? Me and bruh sent some dough every now and then, but sometimes out there a nigga be too busy and might forget for a while. I know you feel me, huh?" he asked.

"Yeah, I feel you, son. That's why a cat gotsta improvise in here, ya dig?" he answered and head nodded to the inmate next to him and to the CO.

KP looked and saw a man kissing a woman, a CO patting down an inmate who was headed back to the yard, and other inmates going back and forth to the bathroom with their women. KP didn't notice anything in particular until he saw the women coming out the men's bathroom. Then it hit him. He smiled and his dad explained how things been working for himself.

"Ya see, son, shit don't change once a nigga hit the yards, feel me? As a matter a fact, shit gets sweeter. I made more money in here than I ever made on the street."

KP added, "What chu do wit the money, though?"

"At first, I was sending it to ya mama. It took me a long time to find out her ass was smokin up all the dope in Peru. Bless her soul, though, but after that, one of my loved ones hooked me up with his wife's sister. And she been runnin for me like Seattle Sue." They smiled as he leaned back in the seat. "Yeah, her ass been kicking these doors down every weekend. I thought you was her at first. But I remembered she had to go visit her relatives in Canada. But yeah, I had her go open me up a bank account overseas. And this been going on for ten whole years now. She brought me a bank receipt up here last week with so many zero's behind the two, I almost fell out my seat wit a heart attack. Now you here, I can finally give you something."

He reached around his neck and unfastened his chain with a cross on it. He then placed it around KP's neck. He kept the other he had for Noonie on. He always wore them for this moment. He finished, "Son, I just have one thing to ask of you. And don't lie." He looked KP dead in the eyes. "Do you use drugs?"

KP was stuck in guilt. He looked away and back. But he never wavered. "Yeah, I do sometimes, but that was because of the stress of my brother. I was by myself, I—"

"That's it, son, that's it, no more. Don't do none a that shit no more. That shit will fuck your brain up and your money. Plus, I'm not giving my dough to no more dope fiends, ya dig? We all we got now, son, and I need to know that shit gon be straight when I get out. You a millionaire now, son."

They both smiled and continued visiting. KP went to the visiting vending machine and bought them some snacks and sodas. While they ate, his dad told him the rundown of how he had the whole black side of the pen on lock. KP told him about Rick getting busted and about the whole war going on between them and Ben-killa. KP's dad told him to fall back and let him send some of his goons to finish the job. But KP already knew that Vick and Jason weren't going to allow that to happen. This was their war and they wanted to end it their way. KP's dad understood that but he still wanted to help bring down one of his rads.

They ate, talked, and scoped other inmates' visitors. They eyed this thick Puerto Rican woman across from them. She had on a too-small blouse that revealed too much of her cleavage. This other couple was having an argument and another couple was playing touchy-feely under the table.

Their two-hour visit had flown by too quickly. KP promised to come back soon and more frequently. This day turned out to be the best either one had in their entire life. The guard had to break them up again from their embrace. And just like that, it was over.

CHAPTER 26

Rick had been arraigned for a double homicide already. His lawyer had already informed him that he would most likely get manslaughter or a possible acquittal. It all depended on the ballistics of the gun that was used to shoot Erica and her survival. Currently, she remained in a coma and the ballistics had not come back yet. Rick's mind had been filled with the hope of recovery for his fiancée and his baby. All he did was work out and read. He recovered 100% from his gunshot wounds and was in full strength. Being in Alameda County Jail was like being in a concentration camp. It was rough, especially if you were a white boy. The brothers and the Mexicans put the full court press down on you, from extortions to beat-downs and rapes. It was rough. Rick was known by all the brothers, so he got a pass. He really didn't care what happened to the white boys who let that type of stuff happen to them. In fact, he even participated in the melees just to let off some steam.

But this one time, he got caught with a group of youngstas putting a smack-down on somebody and he got moved to a different pod. And those youngstas didn't know Rick from the man who guarded them. Rick sat in the day room watching TV. Well, the TV was watching him. He was listening and catching side views of the room full of youngstas talking loud and being extra hyper, slinging their dreds around. He thought to himself that he was too old for this shit. He was so deep in thought that he didn't notice the youngsta come just turn the TV. And not only did he turn it, he stood in front of it, blocking Rick's view. Rick politely asked the youngsta to move.

"Excuse me, little homie," Rick asked.

The youngsta ignored Rick's request. Rick asked again.

"Little dog, could chu scoot over a little bit? I can't see the TV."

By this time a couple of dude's patnas came and stood behind Rick. Rick put his sensors on and balled up his defenders. He already knew where this was going. Rick thought it would make a difference if he told them who he was.

"Uh, man, I'm Rick, man, maybe you heard of me. I be over there on—"

Smack! He couldn't even finish his sentence. One of the youngstas hit Rick in the back of the head.

"Shut the fuck up, peckerwood!" one of the youngstas shouted.

The other one tried to get in on it. "Get his punk ass!"

Rick socked the first one nearest to him. "Mutha fucka!" he shouted.

The one at the TV rushed in and grabbed Rick from the back. His 200-pound body was heavy but his strength was weak. Rick slung the boy around and put the blenders on him, knocked him cold to the floor. The other two charged in simultaneously. Rick caught them both dead on the chin and dropped them. By that time, all the deputies rushed in with pepper spray and batons. All the other inmates scattered for safety while Rick received a face full of spray. He fell to the ground to avoid the Rodney King lesson.

A couple of white officers smiled at the scene. "Somebody finally beat their ass."

They handcuffed Rick and rushed him to the hole. They rushed the other three thugs to the infirmary. Later on that day, Rick sat in his single cell. He felt relaxed finally. Maybe this was what he needed, he thought. Solitude. Some peace from all those knuckleheads. Some time to think about his situation and his girl and baby. Rick had never done what he was about to do. He never thought he would ever in life stoop to this level. He let out a murmuring sigh. He then looked to the ceiling, he got on his knees at the foot of his bunk, and he prayed.

"Lord, I know I ain't never talked to you before, and most likely, you ain't listening to me anyway. But I figured I try this shit—oops—excuse me, Lord, I thought I'd try it out anyway. Right now, Lord, I'm in a serious jam. Not just me, but my fiancée and my baby. I never asked you for nothing ever before in my life. Mainly because I felt you be too busy with other people's problems, and plus you got the whole world to deal with. Besides, I'm a man, and I can handle my own things. But right now, I'm in something I can't handle. And my girl is in something with my baby they can't handle, I need you "

The tears started flowing and Rick couldn't hold them back. Years of held-in tears poured out like a river.

"I need you, Lord, like I never needed you before. You make them well and bring me out of this mess I'm in, I'll go to church every Sunday. I won't miss none, I promise. Amen."

Rick got up off his knees and he felt a relief. He did 100 jumping jacks, 100 sit-ups, and 200 pushups, and went to bed. He lay there on his bunk until he went to sleep.

The next morning he got a lawyer visit. His attorney told him that the ballistics test came back and that the bullets didn't match his gun. The other part was that he had to wait until his next court date to see what he would have to take. The DA told his lawyer that there would be no trial but he still had to cop something. But all that was good news to Rick. Now all he had to do was wait.

CHAPTER 27

S weet Jimmy's was packed. The line for entry was around the block; women in their go-get-'em gear and men in their sharp suits. It was also a lot of regular dressed people too, and it seemed like everybody wanted to be little Jon. Dreds were everywhere. Dreds, baseball caps, and big glasses. The inside of the club was packed, but it also was a party outside. Parking lot pimpin was in full swing. Sideshow traffic was thick and being navigated by Oakland's legal street gang, the police. Each corner held hundreds of spectators. Dudes pulling on girls, vans parked with their side doors open and music slamming. The scene was lovely. Sweet Jimmy's was a club that everybody in Oakland went to on Friday nights. It was located in downtown Oakland off of Telegraph and 17th. It was one of many black-owned clubs in central Oakland. It had been there since the 1970's and by now, old man Jimmy should be a billionaire. Mostly all these people here, their parents used to go to this same club. And now, just like their parents did, they also were doing. But no matter when it was getting done, it was always good to see a group of beautiful people hanging out and having fun. Especially when nobody was getting shot. Getting their ass kicked, now that's a whole different story. This bootsy dude with a scary curl (ancient dude) was getting the smack-down put on him by some youngins. Everybody in the facility seemed to love seeing an old-school ass-kicking.

Little Vick, KP, Ray Ray, and a few other hyphy crew members were standing outside Vick's scraper (his car). Of course they all were strapped. In fact, they were strapped for war. And they all had that in mind too. They didn't care if it was with the police or whoever. All they were going to do was just squeeze first, ask questions last. It did matter who they were looking for, though. They particularly were looking for any person in Ben-killa's crew to come out that front door of Jimmy's; they were gonna light they ass up like the 4th of July. The game was old and didn't nothing change except the faces and places. They knew that some dudes could always get caught slipping coming out of the club. It never failed. The hyphy crew had been moving mean all night. They scoped out a few other clubs already and turned up empty. They saved the best for last.

Vick stood ready as he scanned the crowd. He clutched his semiautomatic Mack 11 as he zeroed in on a familiar face. Instant wrinkles indented his forehead. He sprinted across the street and wedged himself between Shawnie and this dude. Dude was going to jump bad until he saw the handle of the Mack 11 Vick revealed. And by then all the other crew members were at Vick's side. Dude politely raised his hands in surrender and turned and left. Shawnie had the look of cold busted.

"Bitch, what the fuck you doing out here tryin' to shake ya pregnant ass around here for these trick-ass niggas!" Vick griped.

"Um, um, I went to school wit him, that shit wasn't nuthin, he was just—"

Smack! Smack! Smack! Vick slapped the taste out her mouth. He smashed on her party out with the girls instantly. Her girls came up and grabbed her away from Vick's pimp hand. The other boys were laughing and taunting the other girls. Truth was, that dude really did go to school with Shawnie and she wasn't lying. Vick and them had been moving so mean that he really didn't want to hear the truth. He let Shawnie and her girls leave and didn't even care to follow. He was so mad at Shawnie being out there with his seed in her belly. He looked around as he and the crew walked back across the street.

Ray Ray said, "Man, all these trick-ass niggas make it hard for a real playa out here. These niggas ready to buy these hoes a whole house. Trick-ass niggas hate to see how easy it is for a real nigga to get the pussy. I don't buy a bitch shit and I get mo pussy than the law allow." He laughed and other dudes laughed in agreement. And he was right. All those dudes out there on them big rims weren't doing nothing but fronting.

KP was looking at all the fake want-to-be's trying too hard to be something they weren't.

"Actors," KP retorted. "These niggas is straight actors. I bet ain't one of these niggas got or even seen ten stacks before. Bootsy-ass niggas. Probably half of these niggas is snitchin on a real nigga. Niggas turned into straight bitches. I feel like bustin on all these niggas," KP said as he looked on through his glossy eyes.

Vick saw a thick, dark-skinned chick strut past him and he hopped on her. Pretty soon, all the hyphy boys were getting at females walking past. They turned their hunt for the enemies into a hunt for the opposite sex.

"Fuck these bitches, I don't need no hoe, feel me!" Vick shouted. "I ain't in love wit no bitch!"

All the other boys stayed in high pursuit of their female victims. KP's mind was stuck on spraying up the crowds with his semiautomatic Tech Nine. He watched his patnas fall for the traps of the women. Then he grabbed his gun and pointed it at the cars that passed by them. Then he pointed it in the air. And with a devilish grin, he thought, *Watch how I make all these scary mutha fuckas run.* Then he squeezed: *pop pop pop pop pop pop pop pop pop click click click.* He looked at his gun and saw it was jammed, then he tucked it away.

All the crowds scattered like roaches do when the lights come on. All the pretty women practically ran over one another while they tried to make their escape. Cars burned rubber around corners trying to leave. Sharp-dressed dudes ducked and ran for cover. Some dudes even left the women they were talking to. The scene was straight pandemonium. This one dude ran down the sidewalk so fast he almost ran KP over. All he was yelling was, "They shootin, they shootin!" KP burst out laughing. The other hyphy crew members didn't find shit so funny. They all were about to start busting their guns until they saw it was KP doing the shooting. They all filed inside the car and drove off calmly.

CHAPTER 28

Inside the car as it cruised down Broadway, KP was very hyperactive, jumping around, laughing, and praising his narcosis act.

"Did you see all them scary-ass niggas scoot up outta there?" he joked. "I'm tellin you, these niggas out here some bitches!"

"Nigga, that shit was hella stupid," one of the youngstas said.

"Yeah, I know that shit could got all our asses busted," another one stated.

"Yeah, yeah, coulda, woulda," KP retorted. "But it didn't, nigga. I'm finsta go through every hood in Oakland and make all these niggas buy dope from us."

"My niggas Rick and Jay already been already doing that shit, nigga," Ray Ray reminded him.

"Nigga, so what, nigga? Ima do it differently though. Ima pop a nigga first, then make the offer." He smiled at the thought.

Vick drove silently, listening to his patnas talk nonsense. His phone rang and he looked at the screen and saw it was Shawnie's number. He turned the music up a bit so his boys wouldn't hear his conversation, then he answered.

"Yeah?"

"It's me." She spoke softly.

"Hello, I can barely hear you," Vick said.

"I said it's me. I just wanted to make sure you were okay. I heard they was shootin up there." She spoke the concern.

"Yeah, I'm good, just was some stupid nigga," he said as he glanced in the rearview mirror at KP. "I'm good, though. What the fuck was you doing out there and shit when you about to have my baby?"

"It was Nakeya's birthday and she just wanted us to all go hang out. I thought it would be okay since we all ain't been around each other in so long. And the boy was Jamarcus, I told you we went to school together, and I told him I was happy with you. First he thought you was some other nigga at first," she explained.

"Enough, enough, aight?" He cut her off. "Enough about that nigga." He softened up. All that acting like he didn't need a woman earlier was all an act. Because truth was told, he really loved Shawnie. And it was pure jealousy seeing her talking to another dude that made him slap her earlier. Deep down in his heart, it hurt him more than it hurt her. Silence stood between them over the phone, then, *sniffle, sniffle* Vick heard through the phone.

"You okay?" he asked with concern.

"Yeah, I'm fine," *sniffle, sniffle,* she lied.

"You crying, Boo?"

"Naw, I ain't crying."

"I can hear you sniffling. I'm sorry for hittin you, baby."

"You didn't have to go embarrass me in front of my friends like that. I told you I wasn't cheatin on you and I didn't plan to already." *Sniffle, sniffle.*

"Where you at?" he questioned.

"At Nekeya's." *Sniffle, sniffle.* "She getting ready to be wit her dude and—"

"I'm comin to get you. Ima drop these dudes off first, then I'm on my way, okay? She still live in the village?"

"Yeah."

"Alright, just give me bout fifteen minutes, okay?"

"Alright."

"Okay, see you in a minute."

They hung up the phone and Vick went to do just that, drop all they ass off immediately. After making up some drag to his crew, he speedily drove through the back streets to the village and picked Shawnie up. They drove to a hotel and went and made some making-up sex. And with Shawnie in her third trimester, it wasn't all that easy either. But it was very good.

CHAPTER 29

"What's up wit a pimp main?" Jay questioned through his phone. He was riding through traffic on Hegenberger Road. He was on his way to go check up on Erica for Rick. He had talked to Rick earlier and was asked to do so. Right now, he was on the phone with Tyrone. Yeah, Tyrone Taylor. *The* Tyrone.

"Aeh, who dis?" Tyrone asked.

"Oh, it's been that long, huh? You done forgot a nigga voice and shit, huh? Oh, I see."

"Aww, hell naw, I know this ain't my little nigga Jason?" Ty asked.

"Yeah, it is, bruh-bruh, what it do? Why niggas ain't heard from ya ass?" Jason asked, but he already knew why. In fact, the whole town knew why. Everybody knew Tyrone didn't ever have to come back to the town ever again. But everybody knew how the game was. With all its enticements and the addictive behavior of a black man, rich or poor, we still wanted more. It had been years since Tyrone set big FeFe up and plus robbed him and split with his white chick. Tyrone used to front Rick and Jay dope. He was the big homie. In fact, he was the one who showed them the ropes. And it was he who orchestrated the way they should go about taking over the town. Plus, he was the one who really told Pablo to start hooking them up. He and Pablo were very close friends.

"My young homie Jay. You finally got around to calling me back, huh? I thought you forgot me. I hear a lot of good things about you and Rick from our mutual friend. How Rick doing?" Ty asked.

"That nigga in jail for two hot ones," Jay stated.

"What? You playin? What the fuck happened?" Ty was pissed and disappointed.

Jason went on to tell Tyrone what happened with Rick—as much as he could, at least, over the phone. Tyrone offered all his support and then some.

"I can have a team of hitters out there in five hours for y'all. Fuck Ben-killa! And his whole family. Fake-ass old nigga got my little homie caught up over some shit. Just say it, Jay, just say the word and it's done." Tyrone was pissed off to the fullest of pisstivity. But Jay didn't want this big homie to get involved in their mess.

"Naw, T, naw, man, we got this. You got your own shit to deal with, man. It's good, trust me."

"You sho?"

"Yeah, I'm sho, dog, we good. I can promise you that," Jay promised.

"Man, it's good out here outta town, feel me? Market value on used cars way higher, ya dig? And you know how cheap we get cars from the auction. I'm tellin you, Jay, you might wanna come on this side of town," Tyrone reasoned.

"I don't know, man; I might have to think about it, especially with the way things going out here lately. That might be a good idea."

"Well, think about it. And get back at me and let me know the outcome on all those issues. And remember if shit gets too hectic for you, just call me, little bruh, and I'm there."

"Aight, bruh, stay up, one."

"Aight, one." *Click.*

They hung up with one another soon as Jay was parking in front of Highland Hospital. He got out the car and looked up at the tall building with grief. A beautiful assistant desk clerk directed him to the infirmary on the third floor where Erica and her awaited-to-be newborn baby lay in room 315B. He looked in on her and saw she was in a sleepily unconscious state with tubes and IVs hooked up to her. A heart monitor beeped over and over. She still was beautiful even with all the patches on her head and neck. She lay on her back and the lump in her stomach looked like a volleyball. Jay reached over to touch it when a beautiful nurse appeared.

"Um, excuse me, sir, but please don't disturb this patient. And may I ask who you are? Are you any relation to her?" her angelic voice asked.

Jay straightened up and looked at her and said, "Yeah, I am, I'm the baby's uncle and that's my sister-in-law." He cleared his throat and asked, "Are they, are they gonna be okay?"

"Well, as for the mother, it's hard to tell. It's pretty much up to her and of course God, but her surgeries were fine. She's definitely a fighter. Now as for the little one…" She reached and massaged Erica's stomach.

"I thought you said don't—" Jay protested.

"I know, I thought you were a stranger. We get some sickos up in here quite often, but it's okay now since you're family," she finished. "This little guy is gonna be just fine. We call him Mr. Miracle Baby. He's a for sure miracle," she said, smiling.

"It's a him, huh? You sure?" Jay asked incredulously.

"Mister…?"

"Jason, call me Jason."

"Okay, Jason. We know when a baby's a he or she in here."

"Wow!" Jason felt proud like it was his baby. He couldn't wait to see what Rick was going to name him. He stayed and talked with the nurse the whole visit. He found out how far Erica was along in her pregnancy. After exchanging phone numbers with the nurse, Jason kissed Erica on the cheek, rubbed her stomach, and left.

On his way out the door, out of all people to see coming in, it had to be Mrs. Sanchez. Her eyes widened with joy and his narrowed with curiosity. They stopped in the center corridor. There was a brief silence, then they spoke. They gave one another a light hug and they had a brief chat. Jay's little head was speaking to him as he breathed her scent. But his big head took control of the situation. After listening to her explain her reason for being in the hospital, he dismissed himself.

After that encounter with Mrs. Sanchez, Jay felt he needed some loving. And who else could give him that well-rounded package other than his Boo—Nina.

He made it to her apartment in 19 minutes. Since it was Thursday, her Saturday, he knew she'd be home. He hadn't been spending that much time with her lately due to all the issues of his lifestyle. She had started complaining more and more of that. He even stood her up a couple of times on arranged dinner dates. With the excitement of Rick's baby boy on his mind, he was more than ready to share the news with Nina over a candlelit dinner. He parked, made it to the door, and turned the key. He twisted the knob, opened the door, and proceeded through the living room. The house was quiet, nothing unusual about that. But there was stillness about this particular time that made Jay's gut churn. He snatched the 9 mm from his waistband and proceeded with caution.

"Nina? Hey, Boo! You home?" he asked with concern.

Her bedroom door was closed and he heard a little movement from the other side. His heart throbbed and thumped and sank from the thoughts that raced in his head. *What if she's tied up and been raped, what if beaten and raped, what if left for dead—or what if she got a nigga in there?* His mind was playing serious tricks of possibilities on him. He stopped at the door and put his ear to the door, listening for any sound. He heard none. Then the bed wiggled a bit. Then his heart thumped. He grabbed the knob, twisted it, and burst through the door with his gun pointed.

"Ahhhhhh!" Nina screamed. She twisted around from her doggy style position and leaped to her feet. "What are you doing?" she asked hysterically.

He ignored her and started searching the room like a maniac. He searched under the bed.

"Where is he?" He searched in the closet. "Where is he, Nina!" He searched in the master bathroom. "Where the fuck is this nigga, bitch?!" He went back out of the room with Nina in tow, asshole naked. He searched the entire house. No sign of a dude. She lived on the third floor, so hopping out the window was out of the equation. He still checked to see if a nigga was hanging out the window asshole naked. No sign of one.

"What's wrong with you?" Nina questioned out of frustration.

"What the fuck you ass naked for?" he asked.

"I heard you come in, so I got naked to surprise you," she said through tears now. "See, I told you to start coming more so this stuff wouldn't happen. Now look at you. You think I'm cheating on you and

I'm not. And you come here accusing me and calling out my name. You're an asshole!"

She stormed back to her room, crying and her ass jiggling. Jay knew she was pissed off, because Nina never cursed. Something hit Jay like a load of bricks in his heart: Love. This was his wife. He made his mind up right there to pop the question. But first, he had some making up to do. He chased behind her and tried to catch up, but was met with the slamming of the door. And she locked it.

"Nina, come on now, baby. I thought a whole lot of shit—oops—I mean stuff, baby." More silence. He switched the subject. "Rick's having a baby boy. I mean, Erica is for Rick." Silence. He put his forehead on the door and wanted to punch it with his fist. What a fool he was. Nina proved herself long ago that she was real. He should have at least given her the benefit of the doubt.

"Nina, I know you hear me. So I'ma speak, then I'll leave, okay?" Silence. All he heard was sniffles. "Baby, I love you. After seeing Erica laid up in that hospital bed like that today and with my nephew in her stomach, all I wanted was to come home to you and start our own little family. It made me think real hard about life. I never want to hurt you. I never meant to hurt you. Please forgive me. But anyway, to make a long story short, would you give me the honor of being my wife? I promise, I promise I won't—"

Click. The lock unlocked and the door swung open slowly. And there she stood, in all her glory. Smiling with dry tearstains. He reached in and grabbed her and they kissed passionately. She helped him strip himself of his clothing, yet while still kissing she answered his question.

"Yes, yes, baby, I will."

They made love the entire day. And also, the entire night.

CHAPTER 30

*T*here is no pussy better than some pregnant pussy. Vick repeated that thought a thousand times as he left Shawnie at their apartment. His dick was throbbing from her warm tightness. No woman he ever had made him feel like she made him feel. She made him feel like killing up the world and robbing it all of its possessions and placing them at her feet. She had him wide open. Since their quarrel, they'd been spending practically every day together. Plus, she needed him around more to run errands for her. She was due any day now and she wanted him close just in case her water broke. Him being a spot aire, he had to go check his traps. Young Vick was feeling himself. He had his girl on his mind, his music bumping his favorite Tupac song, "Me and My Girlfriend." His whip was shining and so far he collected over six racks off the streets.

He turned the corner on 77th and Bancroft and out of nowhere, *bam!* A car struck him hard head-on into his side door; it hit him so hard it smashed the side inches away from him. The impact knocked Vick out cold. Another car pulled alongside of Vick's car. The back door opened, two masked men jumped out, ran up to Vick, and yanked him out his driver's side window. The driver of the other car that hit him got in the car with the masked men. They put Vick in the middle, got in, and sped off.

Dope fiends and spectators ran to both cars and stole everything of value before the police came. Nobody seemed to be concerned about nothing that took place.

*   *   *

Vick was awakened by two hard slaps to his face. *Smack! Smack!*

"Wake up, sleepyhead," the voice commanded. Vick's eyes were blurry and hazy. Blood dripped from the sides of his mouth. He tried to wipe himself but found he was tied to a chair, hands and feet. His head bobbled and his vision came into focus. Ben-killa looked at him face to face. For the first time, young Vick saw the face of death staring right at him.

"Little boy? Little bitch, you hear me?" Ben-killa asked.

Vick spit a lugie of blood in his face. *Smack! Smack!* Ben-killa's open palm collided with Vick's face. Over the weeks, Ben-killa thought of how he was going to kill Vick. At first, he was about to kill him fast and get it over with. But then, he thought, that would be too easy. So he decided to make Vick suffer. Give his nephew a chance to watch him torture his murderer.

"I see you a little wannabe tough bitch-ass nigga, huh?" Ben asked.

"Fuck you," Vick replied.

"Fuck me? Oh no, playboy, fuck ya bitch. Something you gon wish you was able to do. Where the nigga Jason at?"

"Fuck you, you old-ass, in the way, ass-washed-up bitch." Vick was really working on Ben's nerves.

This torture shit was frustrating him. But to Ben it was all patience. He laughed sinisterly.

"Poor little killa. You can't take the suspense, huh. Yeah, I know." He poured hot grease on Vick's dick.

"AAHHHHH!" Vick hollered.

Being in the abandoned basement, Vick could make as much noise as he wanted to.

"We gon make sure you never use your little friend again," Ben stated.

They had stripped Vick of all his clothes. Ben-killa gave that money to his abiders. Ben-killa grabbed a knife and his cell phone.

"Let's see how much money I can get for your triflin' ass before I kill you. What's ya boy Jay's number?" His greed kicked in as he thought.

"Fuck you," Vick said. *Smack!*

"Shut up, bitch! I already got it. Technology a mutha fucka. You shoulda been using ya brain and maybe you wouldn't be in this mess. Little stupid mutha fucka!" He dialed Jay's number.

After three rings, Jay answered. "Hello!" Silence. "Hello!"

"Jay, don't pay that nigga shit!" Vick screamed in the phone.

Jay didn't understand what that was about. He knew that to be Vick's voice, but he was baffled. He pressed his ear to the phone to hear the background.

Then a whispering voice came on. "Jay, don't speak, just listen. This is your favorite enemy." Ben spoke, Jay listened. "I got cha boy Vick here with me, and it don't look good for him."

Vick hollered in the background from Ben stabbing him in the leg. Then one of Ben's boys duct-taped Vick's mouth. Ben continued to speak in a whisper.

"Jay, you can save our young homie. All I want is one million dollars in two days. The number popped on your screen. Hit me back when you ready. No games." *Click!*

The phone went dead. Jay couldn't believe this nigga was so vicious. Jay had been prolonging and putting off this matter for too long. Now, another one of his little homies was suffering. He knew it could only be Ben-killa. He knew it. But, Jay thought quickly, he wasn't paying that nigga a damn dime. He knew how this shit works. Even if he did pay, Ben-killa would still kill Vick. Jay had played this same game on a couple of people before. It was only one way to ensure Vick's safety.

Jay picked up KP and Ray Ray and headed to Bill's house. Bill was in the living room having a smoker's party all by himself. That coke had him so paranoid, he had all the lights off and kept checking the window every time he heard a car go by. He was standing by the curtain, barely peeking out the window, when Jay pulled up. When he saw Jay, he ran and snatched the door open. Grinding his teeth, he asked, "What's up, Jay, what chu doing out this late? You usually be tucked under around this time."

Jay had to take a step back from the whiff of coke that came pouring out the door. He noticed that Bill didn't want to let him in from the way he stood in the crack of the door.

"Bill man, that nigga Ben got Vick, and it's only one way to save him. Remember what you told me?" Jay waited.

Bill was dumbfounded. He stood stuck. Then, like a bolt of lightning, Bill burst from the door, ran to the back of his house, and came back with a coat on, no shirt underneath, shoes on, no socks, worn-out blue jeans, and a dingy beanie cap. He also had a glass pipe with two extra 25 rocks to share. The pipe still had an unfinished piece of coke in it, still warm. And it reeked.

They hopped in the car and headed to MacArthur Boulevard. Bill navigated from the back seat. He didn't want this to happen and he felt bad, but when it came to love, he had none for nobody but his little homies. He would burn down Oakland and everything in it for them.

CHAPTER 31

Their plan was all worked out before Bill reached Silvia's front door. He didn't have to act the part of being high. He was still high as a kite from moments earlier. Silvia answered her door without caution. Her eyes lit up from shock of Bill's presence. It had been a while since the two last encountered. Bill's eyes did the same when he saw Sil.

"Damn, Sil!" He was taken aback from the new-looking Silvia. She had filled out nicely. She was more illuminating, more radiant. Thick in all the right places, and her skin had a perfect glow to it.

"Damn, Sil, you look good, what you been doing?" Bill asked.

"Bill, thank you, but you know Ben is out now, and you can't be coming by like this. And plus, I stopped anyway."

"You stopped what?"

"I stopped using. I don't do that mess no more, and it look like you should stop too," she said as she looked Bill over.

He was embarrassed, and he felt even worse now for what was about to happen. He convinced her for old times' sake to let him use her house to smoke the remainder of his coke. She did. She led him to the spare room in the back where they used to go a long time ago. He couldn't help admiring the new Silvia. His privates jumped and pulsated for a piece of her. He also held soreness in his heart; he had to figure out a way to get through this situation where she wouldn't be harmed. The plan was to come and torture her, the same way Ben was torturing Vick at this very moment. She closed the door behind him and went to finish watching her TV show.

Inside the room Bill opened the back window for Jay, KP, and Ray Ray to climb in. Her ground-level apartment was an easy target for intruders. They all filed in one by one. Bill's nervousness was a dead giveaway. He was fidgety and repeatedly grinding his teeth.

"A, Jay," Ray Ray said, "maybe we should send Bill back, let him walk back or something. He don't look up to this."

Everybody looked at Bill. KP was even stoned, but he was ready to face any danger head on.

"You do look spooked, Bill. You aight, dude?" KP asked.

"Jay, man, I'm cool, man. I just want ya'll to promise me ya'll won't hurt her, man. She done a lot for me, man, and she ain't one a dem broads that'll call the police on you. So you don't gotta worry about that," Bill said through pleading eyes.

Jay didn't say a word.

"You almost finished in there, Bill? You gotta hurry up, Ben should be here pretty soon," Silvia said from the living room. She had no idea who Ben had pissed off. But being a part of him meant being a part of his lifestyle. She heard the back door open but paid it no mind. She kept her eyes fixed on the television.

"Don't be thinking you can just pop up when you want to—"

Her voice was cut off by the strong forearm grip of KP's arm from the back. He put a sleeper choke on her windpipe and she fell limp in his arms. He dragged her to the back and snatched the phone cord out the wall. Ray Ray tied her up and gagged her mouth. At that time Bill thought it to be good to use Ray Ray's advice and leave. He couldn't stand it no more. He told Jay he was walking back home and to call him and let him know what happened. The guilt of setting her up pounded on him, so he left out of the back window. Jay and them totally understood, and as a matter of fact felt it was better that way. His job was done anyway.

Silvia was awakened by a golden shower from KP's dick. She twisted and turned and hummed until she found that she couldn't escape. She looked around at her captives with piercing eyes and didn't recognize any of them. She realized that Bill had set her up. For what, she didn't know. But it was obvious something serious was going on.

Jay started speaking. "I'm gonna ask you some questions. Answer by shaking or nodding your head, understood?" She nodded up and down. "Okay, good. This really ain't about you, it's about your dude Ben. Your honesty determines if you live or not, understand?" She nodded.

"He is your dude, right?" She nodded. "Is he coming home tonight?" She shook her head no. "Okay, I'ma call him and let you talk to him real quick. If you do well, we'll let you go, and you have to promise you won't go to the police, understand?" She nodded. "I don't want to put a scratch on you, but I will if you make me. Please excuse my friend for the urinal assault on you."

He looked at a smiling KP. He brought him and Ray Ray for the torture part. Jay didn't like to hit women, but those two, KP and Ray Ray, they didn't give a fuck what the gender was on the person they caused harm to.

Jay pulled out his phone and dialed Ben's number. After a couple of rings, Ben answered in a whisper. "So, you got the money that fast, it hasn't even been two days yet—"

He was cut off by an all-too-familiar voice. "Benjamin honey, just do what they ask or they gon kill me."

Silvia's voice broke Ben's hardened whisper and turned it into a panicked shout. "Sil, Sil, is that you? Where you—"

He was cut off again, this time by Jay's calm tone. "Ben, oh Benjamin, how's my man Vick doing?"

"You let her go! Let her go, mutha fucka! She ain't got shit to do with this!" Ben yelled.

He was pacing back and forth, hitting himself with the phone receiver. He didn't think about it being like this. And he obviously underestimated these youngstas.

"Calm down, Ben, calm down, ol' Benny my boy. She do have something to do with this. You know that all fair game in street wars. And everybody is expendable."

"Mutha fucka, if you lay one hand on her, I'll kill everybody that even look like you!" Ben shouted.

"Whoa, whoa now, she's fine—for now at least."

"Ahh, ahh, fuck you!" Vick shouted from the background.

"You hear that, mutha fucka, you hear that? You let her go right now or he's dead," Ben threatened.

Jay closed his eyes and turned and looked at KP and Ray Ray. They knew exactly what he meant. He placed the phone in the air so Ben could hear. At first it was quiet. Then there were screams of pain.

Aggravating piercing hollers and screeching yells. KP had stripped Silvia of all her clothes and left her tied up. He had bent her over and shoved his dope dick in her asshole. And he fucked her really hard. Very hard with hard, torturous, angry strokes. And Ray Ray was pinching her nipples so hard it helped add pain to add to her screams. KP already was attracted to the new-looking Silvia. If he had known the old one, he would have had second thoughts.

"You hear that, Ben? It could get worse if you let it!" Jay stated.

Ben was so mad, he started crying. "Let her go, man, let her go, she ain't did shit, man." He paced around, then he slapped Vick in the face. He now regretted being greedy. He knew he should have just killed Vick quick and got it over with. He didn't think he was messing with some smart vicious youngstas with the capabilities he had.

"I could let her go." He raised a hand for KP and Ray Ray to stop the assault. "I could do that. But you have to let my boy go first. A life for a life."

"Fuck you!" Ben shouted.

Jay raised a hand to KP and Ray to finish the assault. Ben heard the screams of his woman and conceded.

"Okay, okay, alright, man, alright, just let her go, man!" Ben was screaming very vehemently. He was sweating and his boys were waiting for a command. They got one. They were told to untie Vick and drop him off in the parking lot of Highland Hospital.

"His bitch ass is getting dropped at Highland now as we speak. Where's Sil?" he asked with concern and anger in his voice.

"She'll be at home waiting for you." *Click!*

Jay hung up without another word. KP was still pounding away in Silvia's pussy now. Jay shook his head at his wild homies and walked out the room and closed the door. Ray Ray and KP took turns raping Silvia. When they finished, they left Silvia tied up and leaking feces and blood from her asshole and ounces of sperm from her vagina. Her whole body was sore as she lay gagged and tied up on the bed.

Ben-killa's goons did as they were instructed and dropped a bloody Vick in the hospital parking lot. They also were snagged by the sheriff as they tried to speed off. Hospital orderlies and nurses ran out and assisted Vick back inside the hospital.

Ben-killa made it back to Silvia's apartment as fast as he could. When he did, he could see the place was dark. She usually left at least one light on whether or not she was home. She felt that by doing so, she might give a potential burglar an impression that someone was home. Ben-killa drew his gun and stood ready for any surprises. He twisted the doorknob and pushed the door open. Nothing happened. He jumped in the room with his gun pointed, ready to squeeze the trigger.

"Sil!" he yelled. No sound. "Sil!" he yelled again.

Each room he came to, he flicked on the light switch. He heard a muffled voice come from the back room. He flicked the hall light on, his gun staying ahead of him.

"Sil! Is that you?"

"Um, um!" the sound said.

He got to the door and kicked it open. The light from the hallway shined in on Silvia laid out hogtied on the bed, bleeding from her asshole, a puddle of diarrhea-type stool around her and a piece of duct tape over her mouth. Ben rushed and untied her and picked her up in his arms. Tears flowed from both of them as he carried her into the bathroom. He placed her inside the tub and filled it up with warm water. Neither said a word but she displayed nervousness and fear as he showed care and compassion. She reached for him not to leave her side every time he moved. His insides were boiling with hot anger and terrible vengeance for the people involved.

The smell of the burnt coke in the room was a suspicion to him. But he dared not pry. And Silvia dared not reveal her indiscretion with Bill and how she allowed him to use her.

*   *   *

Jay's phone rang twice before he answered it. It was Bill. "Tell me she alive, man, that's all I want to know. Tell me, man."

Bill had been hysterical. He smoked a whole mountain of coke because of the guilt he held inside him. Silvia hadn't never done nothing but show Bill love. She would always give him words of encouragement when Bill would come over her house stressing about his lost family. She would always say, "Just keep the faith, Bill, you don't know what God might do." Bill was hurt. He knew Silvia didn't deserve to be involved with that bastard Ben-killa. Just that thought made Bill want to kill Ben's ass dead wherever he saw him.

"Jay, man, just tell me," Bill cried.

"Only because of you she is," Jay stated.

Jay hung up the phone without giving Bill more detail or without even saying a goodbye. Bill squeezed the phone receiver, dropped a tear, and grinned his teeth. The guilt of setting up Sil was still bearing on him, but a relief she was alive comforted him. He went back to drowning his guilt in 151 Bacardi with no chaser and clouds of Colombian flake hard-rock cocaine.

"At least she ain't dead," he repeated to himself. "At least she ain't dead."

CHAPTER 32

Jay, KP, and Ray Ray rushed over to Highland Hospital to check if Vick was there while Ben-killa rushed to Silvia's apartment to see if she was there. And in the midst of all that, Shawnie was going into labor.

"Oh shit!" she yelled as her water broke. She slipped and slid across the apartment. She held the phone in her hand as she called Vick's number. *Ring, ring, ring!* No answer. She continuously dialed and tried to contact him. She finally gave up on trying to reach him and dialed up her cousin who stayed nearby. He arrived in ten minutes. They packed her bags in his Buick LeSabre and rushed her to Highland Hospital.

"I can't believe this nigga gon be gone somewhere this long and have the audacity not to answer his phone too!" Shawnie said out of frustration.

"That nigga probably out fuckin' another bitch or something, you know how these scandalous niggas be," her cousin hated. He was the kind of cousin that would fuck his girl's cousin if they let him do it. Shawnie hated to have to call on him in her time of need, but he was the one available at the time.

"Shut up, Melvin, you don't know where he at. Just hurry up, my pants are soakin wet!"

"Aight, aight, we almost there."

They arrived there shortly after, and he escorted her to the emergency room. The doctor came out with a wheelchair and seated her in it. He rolled her to the back and placed her in a room. She told her cousin she'd be alright now and she dismissed him. She didn't want to give his nosy ass the satisfaction of looking at her vagina, no matter how nasty all that birth fluid and afterbirth looked. This was her first child, and she only wanted to share that experience with her baby's father. And he was nowhere to be found, in her mind. The doctor gave her a hospital gown and told her to strip. He and Melvin exited the room at the same time.

A few minutes passed and a nurse came in and placed her on the monitor. She had already dilated to 6 centimeters. Her contractions weren't that far apart. And when they came, the whole hospital knew it. Shawnie wanted them to practically overdose her with drugs. They gave her a shot of relaxers to tranquilize her mood, but it barely helped. She wanted the doctor to induce her labor to rush the process but he denied it. She would have to have this baby the old-fashioned way—sober. Her mind raced from Vick to her labor pains and back again. She couldn't believe she was going through this all by her lonely. She was going to kill Vick, she thought, once she got through all of this. His ass had some explaining to do. If he ain't dead already, he was going to wish he was when she got through chewing his ass out. More labor pains came on and broke her thoughts up. The doctor gave her one more shot to stabilize her.

*　　*　　*

Jay, KP, and Ray Ray came rushing into the emergency room. "Vick! Where little Vick at?" KP yelled. He was grabbing hold of doctors and ordering nurses around.

Ray Ray had the common sense to go ask the assistant at the desk. "Excuse me, but could you tell me where I can locate my cousin? His name is Victor Spencer."

"I'm sorry, but Mr. Spencer is being detained for questioning by the Oakland Police. And until they lift the order, I cannot give out any information about him," the sweet little lady stated.

But seeing how frustrated and aggressive KP was being, she did say in a whisper, "He's lost a lot of blood and he'll live. Come back tomorrow at this time, sweetie."

Ray Ray thanked her quietly and went to grab his friends. He told them the news and they accepted it and left.

Vick was being guarded by an officer until he was able to either answer or refuse being questioned. Right now, he was heavily sedated and undergoing surgery. He did lose a lot of blood and had massive puncture wounds. He had a broken collarbone from the car crash and minor head injuries, but he was expected to live. He was laid up unconscious and breathing slow, deep breaths. If only he would have stayed inside the house.

CHAPTER 33

After 20 days in the hole, Rick was let back into the general population. Even though he was still incarcerated, being on mainline was quite liberating compared to the life of solitary confinement. He was let back into the same pod he'd been taken away from. And what would you know, those very same dudes Rick got into it with were there also. Except this time when they saw Rick come in, they were coming up to him with apologies and offers of hands out for Rick. Rick wondered where the big change in their attitudes came from.

An older, clean-cut, gray-haired gentleman came up to Rick. "Excuse me, youngsta… Rick, right?" he asked. Rick nodded his head. "I'm Shocka, I'm from the Guerilla Tribe. I'm chief of this region round here." He extended his hand to Rick and Rick accepted it. He pulled Rick to the side.

"As you know, word travels fast inside these walls. I heard what happened to you. So I got myself and a couple of my rads moved over here as fast as I could."

"And why you do that? I'm not affiliated with nothing," Rick stated in an offensive tone.

"I know you ain't, youngsta, but listen to me first without getting hostile, ya dig?" Shocka replied and then finished. "That's not why we stepped in. Word trickled down from the commander to watch over you and that's why we did. Apparently you got a loved one in your crew and he got a dad who got his arms around all y'all. That's why them little young punks over there doing ten thousand burpies. But shit like that is the least of your worries. By you being white on the outside, the Aryan brothers gon try you when you get to where you goin. My advice to you is to come on home and let us fully embrace you. That way anywhere you go, you have some protection at all times. Just the mention of them three letters will back a mutha up and make 'em think twice."

He stood there and opened his arms for Rick to walk into. Rick thought it over hard and seriously. He knew the OG was right. And he did know that he had a journey ahead. He went against something he vowed not to do. He stepped inside Shocka's arms and pledged his allegiance to the most feared penitentiary gang in history, the BGF.

Right after Rick was taught the secret codes and laws, his name came over the loudspeaker. "McMillian! You have a visit!"

Rick broke away from the protection circle and was escorted by the deputy to the visitor's booth. Jason was already sitting in the visitor's seat when Rick got there. The thick Plexiglas separated them. Rick's eyes lit up from excitement of seeing his crime brother. He rushed to the phone.

"Bruh, what it do?" Rick asked.

"Aw, you know it, man. You lookin lean. What, chu ain't eatin or something?" Jay asked, concerned.

"Yeah, I'm eatin. You think I ain't spendin none-a-dat five racks you put on my books or something?" Rick answered and finished, "Naw, it ain't that. I just got out the hole. Member I told you when I called you last time?"

"Oh yeah, I forgot, that's why you told me don't come see you, oh yeah," Jay stated.

"Yeah, anyway, that shit straight, my rads handled that." Rick let out the cat.

"What you mean, your rads? Don't tell me you up under that act now?" Jay asked, sounding pissed off.

"Be cool over this wire, I'll holla bout that when it's time. Anyway, what's going on out there? Where them naked flicks at you supposed to send?" Rick changed the subject.

"Whatever, nigga, aight. Anyway, they in the mail already, you a get 'em soon," Jay said.

"So you went to check on E for me, bruh?" Rick asked.

"Yeah, I did."

"So what's the news?"

"I got some good news, and some bad news."

Rick's face went from smiles to frowns.

"Good news is E and your son is doing good. E is still in a coma but your son—" Jay said.

"Hold up, you said son? It's a boy?" Rick's face brightened from the news

"You didn't know you was having a boy?" Jay asked.

"Naw, nigga, how was I supposed to know?"

"Yeah, it's a boy, dog," Jay smiled. "So what chu gon name him?" Jay waited.

"What chu think? We already agreed a long time ago to name our first sons after each other, stupid. What, chu forgot?" Rick said.

Jay's face lit up at that. His whole insides tingled. He totally forgot about Rick's decision to join a prison gang.

"So what's the bad news?" Rick asked.

"Young Vick in the hospital. He was kidnapped by dude and tortured real bad. But he gon live."

Rick's face wrinkled up and he gave Jay that look that Jay understood without words. "Kill that nigga Ben-killa fast." Jay nodded.

Rick told Jay when his next court date was and what was going on with his case. The rest of the visit went smoothly and just too fast. Before either one knew it, it was over.

CHAPTER 34

S hawnie sat holding her newborn baby boy. She hadn't named him yet. She left that option up to Vick, although she still hadn't heard from him. The nurse came in and took the baby from her arms and put him in the baby ward. Her belly was throbbing sore from the emergency C-section they had to perform on her. Besides that, the baby was born 7 pounds, 8 ounces and very healthy. Shawnie's mom had driven out here from Stockton. During the pregnancy and its initial stages, Shawnie's mom protested and stood angry with her. But after seeing her first grandson and his beautiful features, she melted from the sight. And when she held him, she didn't want to let him go. Shawnie's mom was one of those mothers who could still get out there and shake with the best of them youngstas. She felt in her mind she wasn't old. She was hip to all the games that men play. And especially the disappearing acts they pull when a woman gets "herself" pregnant. Like she opened her legs, stuck a dildo up in her, and miraculously made sperm come out.

"What kind of nigga is that, leave you to have this baby all by yourself? I told you don't do it long time ago," she ranted and raved. "That's okay though, my grandbaby don't need no deadbeat-ass daddy anyway."

"Mom!" Shawnie yipped.

Shawnie tried to protect Vick's image with her love for him. She knew a side of Vick that nobody else knew. The side that wouldn't do nothing like that. In her gut she felt that something was wrong. It had to be. Vick had never just up and stayed missing this long without calling her. Her woman's intuition just kept telling her that something just wasn't right. And it wasn't.

Little Vick lay on the hospital bed with IVs and tubes going through him, an oxygen mask on his mouth, and heavily sedated. His lacerations were very severe. His status was critical but stable. One of the puncture wounds had struck a main artery in his leg. They had to call a specialist in to perform the tedious surgery. And so far, it had been a success. Only his immediate family had been able to visit with him. His mom and dad hadn't left his side. She had been constantly reading Bible scriptures to him as she sat and watched him sleep. His dad sat and reminisced of times when his son was so innocent. When he crashed into the garage door with his Big Wheel. And when he played Pop Warner football. And he used to come up to his school to watch him play with the other kids. Vick never knew his dad would be watching him. But he was. *Yep, those were the good ol' days*, his pops thought. He never would have guessed in a million years that he would be here watching over his son and hoping he would live. Never once did he fault himself for his son's wrong choice of roads to travel. He knew he had done all he could do for him as a father. He shook his head and dropped some tears for his son.

Back on the other side of the hospital, Shawnie drowned out her mother's patronizing gripe. She followed her gut and started placing calls. She called Jay and got no answer. She called Vick's mom's house and got no answer. She called the police station and found they had no record of any Victor Spencer. She then called the front desk.

"Hello," she spoke.

"Yes, may I help you?" the kind voice asked.

"Yes, I'm calling to see if you have a Victor Spencer listed." The line went silent for a moment.

"Please hold," the voice said.

A minute later, it came back on. "What is it regarding?"

Shawnie's heart dropped with panic. Shock filled her soul. Then worry and concern took over.

"I'm his baby's mother. I'm here at the hospital as we speak, and I just delivered his son. What's going on? Is he alright, what happened, what room he in?" She asked what seemed like a million questions.

"Calm down, calm down, miss. What's your name?"

"Shanaya Jackson."

"What room are you in?"

"215A on the north side."

"Okay." She checked the computer screen. "Okay, Miss Jackson, we do have you here. Now as for Victor Spencer, I can't give you much information, but since you are the newborn mother, I guess you do need to know that. He's being held for questioning after he recovers."

"Recovers from what?"

"Well, he's been stabbed and tortured looks like. I'm not certain but that's the look of it. And I'm sorry but no one is permitted to see him but his immediate family. He's in critical but stable condition. I'm so sorry to be the bearer of bad news, Ms. Jackson."

Shawnie sniffled and tears flowed. The receptionist took sympathy on her and told her what room he was in. But she urged her to not leave her bed unless the doctor said it was okay. And to not even think about going over to Vick's room. Shawnie thanked her for her help and hung up the phone. Her mother stood by and heard the whole thing. She rubbed Shawnie's hand and head, consoling her. Shawnie cried a river worth of tears at the news she just received.

CHAPTER 35

B ill woke up in the morning with a hangover out of this world. He sprawled out on his sofa with his shirt off, sweat causing him to stick to the couch. His jeans were unbuttoned and his private part was hanging out. The empty bottle of 151 was laid on the floor with the top off. A bottle of coco butter lotion sat on the end table next to the sofa. The TV screen displayed a porno flick on pause. A woman in a doggy style position with another woman eating her out stood still. Bill looked around his house at the mess and felt disgusted. He realized that he needed a woman bad. His house was dirty, his clothes were unclean. His kitchen was filthy, his hair was unkempt, and he hadn't had a home-cooked meal in only God knows when. And besides all that, Bill was just flat-out lonely. Sure, he had his share of floozies over the years, and he'd definitely been around the world, and still ain't found his baby.

He got up and went to the fridge. Seeing a few slices of pizza and a half-empty beer, he settled, swigging the beer to help the hangover and popping the slices in the microwave to help his hunger pain. After finishing up the slices, he stripped and took a much-needed shower. He found some decent clothes to sport, then cleaned his house thoroughly. He swept, mopped, washed, and wiped the whole house down. Once cleaned up, he saw that his old house was still beautiful. He remembered times he had his whole family here with him, when his kids were just babies, stair-stepped in age. They had to be at least all married by now, he thought. Life couldn't have felt more real then, more meaningful. Some people live for all the wrong reasons. A car, some jewelry, to be a player, to be fronting around town like a want-to-be gangster, or just to think they're real. And in all actuality, being fake. The real man held a job, took care of his family the right way, came home to his wife every night, lived for his family, pleased one woman, earned respect from his kids by being a father, a provider, took his family to church on Sundays, you know, those type of values. But the dope game came and stripped the communities of all the family values. Especially that damn crack and heroin.

"Shit, shit, shit," Bill cursed himself. He would still have his family right now today if he didn't ever start on the crack.

A knock on the door broke Bill's thoughts of sorrow and self-pity. He was about to open the door precariously, but he didn't want to take any chances. He didn't know what Silvia might have told Ben. But he grabbed his .45-caliber handgun from under the sofa pillow and looked out the curtain.

"Who the fuck is this?" he mumbled to himself.

The people outside on his porch looked like some Jehovah's Witnesses, all dressed up in suits. All three of their backs were to him, and he couldn't see their faces. They didn't give off the impression that they were Feds, so he went to the door and opened it with his gun at his side. He cracked the door wide enough for half his body to be revealed.

"Yeah?" he asked annoyingly.

The three faces that stared back at him looked identical to his. His body froze and his eyes widened. His hand dropped the gun he was holding to the floor. It made a loud clanging sound when it fell. The three faces smiled as they said, "Dad!" Bill's eyes instantly filled with water and spilled over his face. His heart was pounding with nervousness. He forgot to even invite them in.

"Are you gonna let us in or what?" the shortest of the three asked.

"Yeah, yeah, excuse me, come on in, y'all, come on in. Damn, I can't believe this," Bill expressed.

As each one came in, he gave them a long hug. All were taller than he. And he couldn't make out who was who. It had been a long time since he saw them. He knew their names but looking at them, it was hard to differentiate. And it showed on Bill's face. They saw the confused look Bill expressed and answered his unasked question.

"I'm Wayne," the smallest one said.

"I'm Walter," the tallest one said.

"And I'm William Jr.," the middle height one said.

All three smiled at the joyous look on their father's face. The tears kept coming down Bill's face like a waterfall. He couldn't believe this day finally came around. Something in Bill's insides made him feel like he had additional body parts. He started feeling his chest and stomach. The tingles were everywhere on him.

"Where's y'all momma at? How she doing?"

All three looked at each other sadly. Then Jr. answered.

"She passed a couple months ago. She had a brain tumor and the doctors couldn't reverse it."

Bill felt a pang in his chest; he still loved his ex-wife, and he felt very bad about the news.

"So, how y'all been holdin up? Y'all look okay, but are you alright?" he asked no one in particular.

"We've been cool, Pop," Walter answered. His voice was the deepest out of the three. "I just graduated from Morehouse College and just accepted a basketball contract for the Warriors," he smiled.

Bill felt proud to hear that. Then Jr. spoke. "I went to law school and passed the bar, and now I'm a criminal law specialist. I'm not with no firm yet, but I do a lot of freelance work on the side. Luckily the world is full of criminals or else I'd be broke out here."

He and Walter looked at Wayne with disappointed eyes. Bill wondered what that was for.

"So, what about you, Wayne? What you got goin on these days?" Bill asked.

Wayne was the youngest. His mother and brothers considered him to be the black sheep of the family. She would always tell him how much he reminded her of his daddy. And he took that to heart. In fact, he loved hearing it. He felt that was his only attachment he had to his biological father. So over the years he got into more and more trouble. He had been in an unnumbered amount of shootings. And he ran a criminal organization in Atlanta. He was feared by almost the whole eastside of the city. He didn't want to tell his dad all that, so he just said, "I've been cool, Pop. I'm straight."

Bill saw right through all that. His son's swagger was a dead giveaway. But Bill didn't pry into it; he left it at that. They enjoyed one another like they always been around one another. The chemistry was dynamic.

Wayne looked at the gun on the floor and asked, "What chu need that for, Pops, you got some problems?"

CHAPTER 36

B en-killa was furious.

"These little niggas must don't know who the fuck I am," he said, talking to himself. He sat on the living room couch stuffing Teflon shells into a hundred-round clip of an AK 47. Sweat poured from his body.

"These mutha fuckas just don't know!" he shouted. "I laid this shit, I was born in this shit, not sworn in it! I been killin niggas out here!" He spoke to himself as if speaking to another person. Silvia had been laid in the bed for a couple of days now. From the other room she could hear Ben ranting and raving and carrying on.

"Benjamin, you call me? What chu say, honey?" she asked.

When Ben took her to the hospital, they saw that nothing was wrong with her. After checking her out, they gave her some antibiotics, some anti-inflammatories and painkillers, and put her on bed rest. Neither she nor Ben wanted the police involved, so they lied and said they had rough sex with one another. Ben wanted to handle this all by himself.

"Nothin, I wasn't talkin to you, Sil," he answered apprehensively.

She knew he was up to something no good. They had already talked about it. She tried to talk him down, but to no avail.

"Ben, Ben darling, please, just wait, please, at least until I'm well. I told you I don't know who set me up, I told you to just wait," she pleaded.

"You don't tell me shit, woman!" Ben hollered.

"I just want to go with you. I just feel like you need some extra eyes out there with you. My gut don't feel right, baby, please don't go out without me," Silvia cried.

"Sil, I can't let no shit like this just ride by like that. You can't let shit like that slide for too long. I waited long enough. One a them little bastards gonna get it. They violated big time. They raped you, baby. They fuckin raped you!" He popped the clip in the rifle as he stood.

Silvia was so anxious to get up and get out the bed and go with him, she cried. Her ass was still sore as well as her body. Ben dressed up in army camouflage gear like he was going to war in Iraq. Silvia's gut twisted and turned as he dressed. She begged and urged him to just stay with her. Revenge clouded his mind of rational thought. Nearby sirens could be heard, and the sounds of the night seemed full of activity. The night was young and the streets were old, and it's nobody more worse than a young dummy except an old fool. And the town was full of both.

Ben walked in the room with Silvia and knelt down and kissed her on the mouth. She eagerly wrapped her arms around his neck and held on tight. She felt something strange in that hug. He pried his neck loose and turned away. As he left out the door of the room, Silvia whispered, "I love you."

Ben had his AK 47 at his side under his trench coat. His bulletproof vest brought out his physique. Inside his mind he continually repeated a scripture: "Vengeance is mine, says the Lord. I will repay." His mind kept saying it over and over and over. But he didn't take heed to the hint.

He stepped onto the porch and closed and locked this door behind himself. He stood there for a moment, breathed in the night air, and looked up to the stars. His eyes were brought back down to the red dot on his chest. His reaction was too slow; the bullet pierced straight through the vest. *Pow!* Then one after another, they came pouring into his body. He tried to escape by running, but the shooter had perfect aim with the red dot target. Everywhere Ben tried to run he was met with a barrage of bullets. Under the mask KP smiled demonically at the sight. Ben's AK 47 fell to the side, never used.

Silvia heard the shots from her bedroom and her heart sank. She knew it was Ben, she just knew. She hopped out of bed, ignoring her aches and pains. She dashed to the front in a panic. After fumbling trying to unlock the door, she finally succeeded. Her scream pierced the air.

"Ahhhh! Nooooo! Ben!" She ran to Ben, oblivious to the shooter still shooting Ben as he lay there jerking from the shots he received. As she reached out to Ben, she grabbed the assault rifle. As she grabbed it, another masked man walked up calmly behind her. KP stopped shooting and stood there smiling under his mask. She tried to pick up the heavy rifle, and she did. Ray Ray let her squeeze the trigger. Nothing happened. The safety was on. Ray Ray raised his gun with the red beam landing on her forehead. And with a devilish grin he fired two shots into her head. He also walked up to Ben and fired two shots into his head.

All the neighbors in the apartment watched the two masked men flee into the night. Silvia lay there over top of Ben, she and he bleeding to death in the sight of their neighbors. Jay's plan worked out smoothly. Jay knew that all along. He knew that attacking Silvia in the first place would draw Ben-killa right into the trap. And it worked. Killing Silvia was his way of doing clean work. He felt sorry he had to break bad on his silent promise to Bill, but Jay knew he couldn't take any chances. *It's already too bad we've got to deal with bitch-ass niggas. But these bitches will tell on you even faster.* Jay thought that all the time. He always remembered things his OG folks Tyrone told him. And besides, KP and Ray Ray nagged at it every day after the rape.

As for Ben-killa, some might call what happened street justice. All his years of tormenting the street finally caught up to him. Some might say the game god repaid him. At one point in his life, he would probably agree to that. But now, he most likely would have said that he should have listened to those signs, when Silvia pleaded for him to stay put and when God forewarned him in his own mind who will repay his vengeance.

CHAPTER 37

L ife was bittersweet for Jay. He brought Bill's son Wayne in on the movement of all the coke he was getting. It was perfect timing too. With Rick gone it was hard for Jay to make other moves. He trusted a few people in the crew, but mostly all the crew did some kind of drug or drank too much. He had love for them, but being a boss meant being responsible and a good manager. If you couldn't even manage yourself, how were you going to manage somebody else? A mind's a terrible thing to waste, he would say. That was his motto, what he lived by. And mostly none of his youngins were ready to grab the torch if need be. He felt a blessing when Bill introduced them. And from there it had been even more proven to be.

It had been three months now. Rick was about to be sentenced; Erica was due any day now. She was still in a coma, but still alive. And little Vick was paralyzed in the left leg. Jay sent him and Shawnie to stay in the house in Atlanta with their newborn baby. Vick sat at the house all day, guarding the hundreds of keys in the house that Wayne came to move once a month. Vick's private tool was saved also. Retardedly ugly, though, but it worked. Rick's lawyer made a deal for a plea bargain. Rick's guilty plea got him a double manslaughter. He was happy with that; at least he got a release date, he thought. Bill stayed mad at Jay for a little while but soon forgave him for killing Silvia. All he could do was chalk it up to the game. Shit happens.

Jay's wedding was tomorrow so he took the day to make last-minute preparations. He didn't want anything to go wrong. He wanted everyone to wear all white. He had a special decorator come and bring out the image of heaven. The wedding was being held at the Church of Christ, Rick's momma's old church. Rick's place as best man was filled by Bill, and he felt honored. Only a select few were invited, but the whole crew would fill the place.

Bill and Jay stood in the tuxedo store being refitted for their suits. "Jay, man." Bill ground his teeth. "I ain't been this damn sharp since me and ex-wife's wedding." He thought back to the day a brief moment.

"Yeah, I see you over there lookin shinier than a brand new three-dollar bill," Jay joked.

"I feel that way too, man. Thanks for letting me be the best man, Jay. You don't know how much this mean to me. It seem like just the other day I saw y'all sleepin on my living room couch. Now I'm watching y'all do grown-man shit. Man, time sho do fly by fast. Y'all makin me feel like a old-ass man," Bill stated.

"Naw, man, you ain't old," Jay smiled. "You look about ten years younger with that new haircut."

The tailor was working the measuring tape as they were talking. Jay never thought the day would come when he would be getting married. But he knew Nina was worth it. And what better time to do so when things were going smooth. When he broke the news to Rick, Rick was happy for him.

"It's about time, nigga. I told you you shoulda been locked Nina down. I'm happy for you, bruh." Rick's tone saddened and Jay could hear the difference in his tone.

"What's wrong, bruh, you aight up in there?" Jay asked with concern.

"Yeah, I'm straight, bruh. I just wish I was there with you to help you celebrate, that's all. When I get back in about twenty years, we can do it then." He smiled, trying to add a joke in on himself. "Just make sure you send me some pictures of everybody."

"No doubt, you already know them coming, bruh." Jay paused. "I miss you, bruh."

"I miss you too, bruh."

When the call ended, Jay felt sad. Sometimes he wished it was him in there locked up instead of Rick. He vowed that his brotha from another motha wouldn't want for nothing, and he made sure that he saved double for him and Rick.

Jay snapped back to where he stood with Bill. Bill looked good since he stopped smoking coke. Jay smiled and admired him.

"Rick would sho love to see you now," Jay stated to Bill. "I always knew you could do it, Bill. I'm proud of you, man."

"Thanks, Jay," Bill stated.

The tailor was just about finished with the both of them. He was putting the final measurements on the sleeve of Bill's arm.

"I'm so thankful that I was blessed by the Lord by seeing my sons again, man. I had to do something in return to show my appreciation. But yeah, I wish Rick was here too, man. I think his lawyer could have got him self-defense though if he woulda went all the way to trial. My opinion, I think he fucked him over."

"Yeah, I thought about that too," Jay answered. "That's why we fired his ass and we got your boy Jr. on his appeal already. Who knows, he might be able to get that sentence reversed. I hope so. I miss my bruh to death!"

They finished and went and ran some more errands around town, then spent the rest of the day preparing for tomorrow.

CHAPTER 38

The Wedding

T he outside of the church building was decorated in fine heavenly ornaments. Cars were lined back to back and double-parked. There were all sorts of expensive rides and luxury sedans. A space was reserved for the two limos, one for the groom and one for the bride and their entourage. People hung out front in groups of twos and threes, socializing with one another. Everyone was dressed up in all-white linen attire. The scene was beautiful. The preacher was inside greeting all the guests as they arrived and keeping them entertained with a sermon. All the pews were full of guests and family. Nina's mom and dad flew out here from Texas with her sister and little brother. Her dad wouldn't have missed this for the world. He always wanted the honor of walking his oldest daughter down the aisle. Nina looked like a mixture of both her parents, except she had her mom's height, and her sister and brother the same. Her mom and dad were good, wholesome folks who lived a moderate life. Nina had gotten accepted in UC Berkeley a while ago and she had to move to California. When she got down here, she got so used to the life of the West Coast that she stayed. Thanks to her mom and dad's upbringing of her, her morals and values stuck with her. Only thing, she had a yearning for dudes like Jay. And when she met Jay, she was stuck. Jay was all she ever needed in a man and more.

Jay and his crew of groomsmen arrived first in their limo. The limo driver parked and opened the door for Jay and his immediate eight-man crew. Little Vick's crutches exited first, then himself; he hobbled along on the crutches and stood by the door. The crowd had parted like the Red Sea for their crew. Ray Ray came and stood by Vick; KP came by them. All three were strapped up under their tuxedo coats. Next, all three of Bill's sons exited and came and stood by KP and them.

Bill stepped out next, looking and feeling dapper, and it showed all over his face. He had a right to be; Jay was like his adopted son. He felt honored to be a part of his wedding, something he always wanted to do with his real sons. But with Jay being close to him all these years, it still felt the same. He looked down the row of finely dressed men who, in some way or another, he had a hand in helping raise all of them at some point in their lives. They were all dressed alike in their tailor-made-to-fit tuxedos.

KP's dreds were pulled back into a ponytail. Vick had cut his off. He wore a wavy Caesar cut that accentuated his complexion better. Ray Ray still had his dreds. He just let them hang loosely. Being the shorter of them all and the youngest, he purposely made his dreds swing with every turn of his head for attention. Bill smiled and grinned his teeth. He turned back to the limo as Jay stepped out.

Jay's tuxedo was designed slightly different from the others but still it fit in sequence. He stood at the door of the limo in admiration of the scene. He leaned over and asked Bill, smiling, "You got the ring, old man?"

Bill whispered back, "I ain't old yet, my memory ain't that bad." He tapped his breast pocket to reassure Jay he had it there.

The photographer snapped unlimited shots of them. Jay led and they filed in suit behind him in the building.

Inside the building was decorated with life-like angels hanging from the ceiling, clouds and stars as well. Everyone came to order and started clapping their hands as Jay approached the altar. The preacher stood smiling with the Bible in his hand. Everyone took their positions. No later than soon as the groomsmen were positioned, the flower girl came down the aisle, throwing flowers in front of her. The bridesmaids came down behind her, all dressed in beautifully designed dresses, all alike. Everyone stood up and fell silent.

The organ player started the marching bride music. Nina entered in on her father's arm. Tears fell from her face. Her train on her dress was so long it took four little girls to carry it, two on each side. She was beautiful! Jay stood at the altar looking at his wife-to-be approaching him. She looked so gorgeous to him. It seemed like a lifetime passed by as long as she took to reach him. When she finally did, the preacher gladly started the ceremony.

"Who is it that gives this woman to be married?" he asked while looking at Nina's dad. The preacher was a dark-skinned, gray-haired, heavy man with gray sideburns, a very jolly man.

Nina's dad proudly answered, "I do."

The preacher proceeded and after they said their special vows to each other, they each placed their rings on each other's fingers. Vick and Shawnie stood facing one another with thoughts of marriage ringing in their eyes. KP stood eye to eye with one of Nina's sorority sisters, thinking about how he was going to beat her pussy up later with his dope dick. A smile surfaced his face and so did she, like she knew what he was thinking. She was a cute thing too. Light brown with nice eyes and a big booty, his type.

All of a sudden, right after the preacher gave his blessing to kiss the bride, the band started up with the music to Luther Vandross's "Here and Now." And guess who was singing it: Ray Ray. He had all the girls in a daze and all the dudes in amazement. Looking at him, nobody would suspect him to sound exactly like Luther Vandross. I mean, he hit every note exactly right. The whole church was on fire; all the girls were in tears and even some of the dudes. Jay even dropped some tears with Nina in his arms from the lyrics of the song. Ray Ray sang the shit out of that song. He had the girls' panties wet when he finished. The photographer took thousands and thousands of pictures. Jay went all out, he spared no expense.

The reception was held at the Hilton, of course. And as usual, the whole first and second floors were bought out. Folks from out of town had not a worry or inconvenience at all. Everything was paid for. Everyone got drunk as a skunk. R-Kelly's two-step came on and all the old-timers were trying to do the electric slide. Jay and Nina had a scheduled flight to catch in about two hours. They had decided to go honeymoon in Jamaica. Nina always wanted to go there ever since she was little. After she and her father danced, she and Jay boogied across the floor. They tired themselves out with the old-school moves they were doing. Bill and his sons each had a fine sister on the floor getting their boogie on. Bill had met a nice church-going sister after the wedding and they'd been hitting it off so far.

Everyone formed a line and presented their money gift in envelopes to Jay and Nina in their gift basket. The Sanchez family was there and Pablo had Mrs. Sanchez go deliver their family gift to the basket. Jay and Pablo locked eyes with a respectful nod and a smile. Little Pap held up a glass of wine to Jay and took a sip. They smiled at one another also. The gift basket was already full of envelopes and it was only half the people's gifts. A fine-ass white woman walked up to Jay. Jay had been taking notice of her even at the wedding. He had never seen her face before, but she was so gorgeous one couldn't help but notice her presence. Her glow stood out illuminating. Her all-white silk gown hung to her perfectly curved body as she stood in front of Jay and Nina's table. She then sat down by Jason. Jay had a poignant expression on his face, while Nina was stoic. Nina then asked indignantly, "Excuse me?"

"I'm sorry, but my feet are killing me," the white woman stated, then she finished, "Oh, I'm sorry, I'm Karen." She held out her hand to each of them, who accepted it out of good manners. Then she finished, "Jay, your friend Tyrone sends his love and his apologies for not being able to make it. So, he sent me all the way out here to represent him."

Jay's apprehension eased at the mention of his OG patna Tyrone's name. He still didn't know this white woman but he figured she must be FeFe's ex-wife that Tyrone stole and ran off with, after they robbed FeFe of his bread a while ago. Then, he understood it all. Nina was still kind of baffled but she ran along with her husband's lead. Jay introduced Nina and he and Karen commenced to talking about Tyrone.

"Oh, he's fine, Jason. He and I just not too long ago tied the knot ourselves." She flashed her 18-karat wedding ring with a smile.

"Oh yeah? Well congratulations to you," Jay said.

Karen leaned in closer and said, "Tyrone said to tell you to be careful and stay alert. He says that you are not State material no more, now you are Fed's. He said to be smart and shut down for three months every year. It throws them off balance."

"Yeah, that's real, that's what's up," Jay answered.

As they talked, Jason could see how Tyrone fell for Karen. She was absolutely beautiful. Jay looked at his watch and saw that he and Nina had an hour before their plane left. He and Karen had been talking for about 45 minutes, Nina nudged him as a signal for them to leave. Karen had to leave too; her flight was 90 minutes after theirs. Two different destinations. They said their goodbyes with light hugs and Karen departed. Jay and Nina still had people to say goodbye to.

Bill approached Jay and Nina as they were exiting their table. He had his new lady friend, Emma, on his side. "Hey, Jay I'ma be takin off, man. Me and my friend here are gonna try and catch us a late flick." He introduced her to Jay and Nina and they split. Jay had appointed Bill's son William Jr. to take care of the money bag. The Sanchezes had already left and Nina's parents had gone to their rooms already. Nina said she'd call them from the limo on the way to the airport. KP and Ray Ray had their hands full with all the women's asses on the dance floor. The music was blaring through the speakers. Jay glanced over at the bar and he thought about just last year when Rick had reunited with Erica right at that stool. Thinking about them both—well, all three of them, including the baby—brought a distant look upon his face. Nina noticed.

"What's wrong, baby?"

"Aw, nuthin, Boo, just thinking about my boy Rick, that's all."

"Ohhh, baby," she said as she wrapped her arms around his waist and laid her head on his chest. "It's going to be okay, baby. Just leave it all in God's hands, baby. He'll fix it."

They walked through the crowd to the exit and left the party to their flight.

CHAPTER 39

Erica's eyes fluttered speedily and rolled into her head. The heart monitor beeped rapidly. Her moans and groans became intense. Her head turned back and forth and side to side. Her moans became piercing screams, "Ahhhhh!" She twisted and squirmed in her hospital bed. Her hand knocked the IV over to the floor. The nurse whom Jay had the conversation with when he came to check on Erica came running into the room.

"Oh my God!" she gasped with her hand up to her mouth. "Doctor! Doctor!" she called out loudly as she ran to Erica's side to try and stabilize her. The nurse, whose name was Samantha (but she preferred to be called Sammy for short because that was her deceased father's name), placed her smooth caramel hand on Erica's forehead to check her temperature. Erica was burning hot! Erica was still in a semiconscious state. She continued to squirm and twist uncontrollably. Sammy lifted the covers and saw the Erica was soaking wet down there. By then, doctors and other nurses had entered the room in a frantic frenzy. The doctor was ordering the nurses around speedily.

"Hook this, plug that, give me those, and give her this."

One of them injected Erica with a long needle full of anesthesia. Erica immediately stabilized and breathed easily. The baby monitor had shown that she was centimeters overdue. That baby was already traveling down. Erica must have been dreaming or something because she was now back in sleep world. Sammy stood by, rubbing a cold towel on Erica's forehead to keep her cool. She had been the nurse assigned to watch over Erica and the miracle baby, and she'd been doing so for months now. She had grown closely attached to her patients and she stayed, praying for her and the baby's survival. Sometimes she even pulled double shifts to make sure they were receiving the proper care.

She looked on Erica with great sympathy and compassion. Then she kissed the top of Erica's forehead.

The doctor was preparing to perform an emergency C-section. Erica mumbled something that took them by surprise, especially Sammy. She alertly grabbed Erica's hand and place her ear as close to Erica's mouth as she could. Then she spoke. "Erica? Erica honey, I hear you, I'm here with you, dear, as always. It's me, it's me, Sammy, you hear me?" Samantha asked and spoke to Erica as she always had been when she'd come and sit with Erica for hours at a time, talking to her. She held on to that hope for her. And now, it revealed a taste of it. Erica squeezed Sammy's hand. Tears were flowing now down Sammy's face. They were dropping onto Erica's cheeks and on her head. Erica's eyes started to flutter again. Then she mumbled something again.

The doctor stated, "Keep talking to her," as he continued with the surgery.

Sammy continued, "E, it's me, honey, it's Sammy, your new friend. Come on, honey, you're gonna be fine. Open your eyes now, dear. Fight it, E, be strong, fight."

Erica's eyes stopped fluttering and she calmed back down and went back into a stupor. Her hand relaxed in Sammy's hand and she breathed lightly. She breathed lightly as she murmured lightly also. The doctor now held the head of the baby boy, whose red, curly hair stuck out of Erica's vagina. Other nurses wiped up the excess blood and feces that littered around the bottom of Erica. Some were keeping a close watch on the monitors and were monitoring the heart rates of both Erica and the baby. The baby was fine and breathing regularly. The monitor revealed that he had a slight heart murmur but he was fine. It was Erica's machine that caused them to study it with more concern. Hers was weaker. It was way below the healthy beat of a human heart. Instead of beating every second, it beat every other second. *Beep-beep* pause, *beep-beep* pause, *beep-beep* pause. They admonished Samantha to administer oxygen to Erica to help her breathe easier. She did. Erica was in such an induced stupor state of consciousness that she didn't even feel any pain at all. She was well in labor, yes. But she was in labor without the labor pains. And that was a blessing to her. A rarity. Something unheard of. Well, not in a regular convo at least. Usually in a situation like this, one of the patients' lives will be sacrificed for the other's survival. And it was usually the mother's. In this particular case, it was different. Erica had a very good percentage of pulling through this with her life as well.

Inside her mind she was dreaming of all the good times she and Rick shared and of the wedding they were preparing and hoped for. She saw herself walking down the aisle in her white dress beautifully adorned, with her son and Rick waiting for her at the altar. Everything was a blur in her mind. Her eyes fluttered and this time she spoke as if Rick was right beside her.

The doctor had the baby halfway out as he held the bloody baby, twisting him out of Erica. The nurses kept their eyes on Erica's heart rate monitor screen. Its beep slowed down again. *Beep-beep-beep-beep* pause. The doctor urgently spoke to Samantha for her to check the oxygen machine to see if it was anything obstructing the air flow. There was nothing.

Sammy had tears of worry streaming down her pretty almond-colored face. Her thin brown eyes were red from her crying. She spoke softly. "Rick is not here, Erica sweetie, but he's waiting for you. He loves you very much and he needs you to pull through this," she consoled Erica genuinely.

The doctor had the baby out now, and he was clearing all of his breathing pathways and cleaning the baby off. The baby let out a loud cry: "Whhhnnnn!!" At the same time, Erica's monitor went flat. *Beeeeeep!* The doctor quickly handed the baby to a nurse. The other nurse cut the umbilical cord speedily and patched the baby up. The doctor rushed to Erica's side and administered CPR. He pumped her chest with his hands. Breathed into her mouth, checked her pulse, and listened closely to her face. Nothing. He tried again. Pumped, breathed, pulse. Nothing again. Pumped, breathed, pulse. Same thing. He then grabbed the electric shock paddles.

"Clear!" *Shock!* "Clear!" *Shock!*

Erica's body jumped from the electric shock treatment. Still no response. The doctor looked around at all the crying faces and shook his head in defeat. Another tragic and lost cause.

Samantha leaped at the electric shock paddles and snatched them from the doctor's hands. Everyone gasped with shock from her sudden move. She refused to let her hope go. Her faith was too strong to just give up so easily. She hurriedly applied the gel to the paddle, clapped them together. "Clear!" her trembling voice hollered out. *Shock!* The monitor beeped. *Beep!*

The life of the machine drew everyone's unbelieving attention. *Beep, beep, beep, beep, beep, beep.* Erica breathed in deeply and everyone in the room turned to joy. Hallelujah's and thank-you Jesus' were whispered through the room. The doctor applied a manual breathing ball to her mouth and squeezed air into her mouth. Samantha tossed the shock paddles to the side, grabbed a wet towel, and placed it on Erica's head.

Erica's eyes opened up fully wide in bewilderment. Her hand reached up and weakly touched the object over her mouth. She was now breathing more strongly on her own. She asked softly, "Where am I? What's going on?"

The doctor shushed her, and Sammy answered her question. "You're in the hospital and you just came out of a coma after six months."

Erica immediately remembered the sound of Samantha's voice. "I heard you." She paused, then finished, "I heard you when you used to talk to me. But I couldn't answer you." Then she remembered with urgency. "Where's my baby?!" She felt her stomach.

The doctor interceded. "Your son is fine. He's—"

Erica cut him off. "Son? Where is he? Is he—"

The doctor cut her off this time. "He's fine, he's fine."

He then ordered the nurse to place the child in Erica's arms. Erica's face overflowed with tears. The doctor was amazed at how alert and responsive that Erica was. He thought for sure that she would more than likely be a vegetable. But the good God seemed to be shining his light down on her. Her memory even seemed to be functioning intact. She looked to Sammy and asked her could she call Jason for her. Samantha already had the number programmed in her phone, so she stepped outside and called him.

CHAPTER 40

J ason and Nina were enjoying the warm sun beaming down on them. This was one of the happiest days of their lives, especially Nina's; you know how women are about marriage. She had her arm wrapped under Jason as they lay on top of the lounge chair. Jay had put it down on her in the bedroom of their suite from the time they checked in until all through this morning. They ate breakfast and decided to go catch some sun rays and sip martinis on the beach. Nina got that idea when she looked out the window this morning after breakfast. Besides, her pussy was throbbing anyway and she wanted to give it a break also. They had two whole weeks to make as much love as they desired. Plus, by this being their first time in Jamaica, they wanted to see the clear blue waters and all the pretty exotic fish.

Jason couldn't have been feeling better than he already was. He was rich, everything was going his way, his crew was cool, his worst enemy was gone, he had his wife at his side, and the rest of the world to conquer if he chose to do so. With the exception of his brother Rick being in jail, all else was perfect to him. He stared off into the ocean, looking past all the people on boats and wind surfing, all the swimmers and curious children playing in the near waters.

Nina noticed his distant behavior, his far-off company, and she asked playfully, "Hey, you. Is something the matter, honey?" Full of concern, she squeezed herself into him.

He obliged and wrapped his arm around her and sighed. "Ahhh, nothing's wrong, baby. That's what's wrong. Everything is perfect. And you know what that means?" he questioned her, but not really looking for an answer. He answered his own question. "That means that something's wrong, or something's about to go wrong. Things are never this perfect in the life I'm living. It's always something wrong." He paused. "You know, my Uncle Tyrone told his wife to tell me something and now that I think about it, I really feel that he's right."

"And what's that?" Nina questioned.

"He said that I was Fed material now and that I should slow down. And my gut tells me that that is what it is time for me to do. Just kick back and spend some of this money we got and build our family."

Nina smiled at that part and snuggled closer. "Now that's what I'm thinking too, the making the babies part," Nina stated.

They both grinned at the notion. Then Jay's phone rang out loud—*ring, ring!* He looked down at the caller ID and saw the name "Samantha" displayed. He felt embarrassed, kind of cold busted. It took him a minute for the name to register in his mind. Nina was watching him with curiosity as to wonder why he wasn't answering his phone. Jay was a happily married man now. And he didn't want to start off his married life keeping secrets and cheating on his wife. When it finally hit him as to who this was calling him, the phone had stopped ringing. Although Jay was attracted to Samantha physically, and he would have hit those skins if she let him, he knew that he told her to call him if there were any changes whatsoever in Erica or the baby's condition. So now, he sat up straight with a panic.

"What's wrong, baby? Who was that?" Nina asked, herself worried now.

"That's the hospital," Jason answered, now worried to death as to what's the matter. He stared back at the phone in hopes for it to ring again. It did. *Ring, ring!* This time he answered immediately without hesitation. "Hello, hello?" He held the phone to his ear. "Yes, um, huh, of course, sure, no problem. Yes, I'm fine, thank you. Um-hmm, um-hmm, yes, um-hmm, yeah! Hey! Alright! Tell her we'll be there first thing tomorrow morning. Tell her to hang in there, tell her I also have a surprise for her too," he said while looking at Nina, then he finished, "Thank you for callin, Samantha, I really appreciate it. Okay, take care, see you tomorrow, bye-bye."

Jason hung up the phone on a joyous emotion. That was it. That was the last sign he needed for him to stop or lean back for a minute.

Nina watched him eagerly with anticipation, wanting to know the news, although she heard bits and pieces of it.

"Well?" she asked.

"Well, let's go pack up our shit, we're leaving. Erica just had my nephew and she's out of her coma." And that was that.

CHAPTER 41

R ick sat on his bunk just staring up at the ceiling. Actually, he was lying on his back doing so. He moved in a cell with the OG homie Shocka. Rick was treated like straight family from his prison loved ones. He was able to let out his frustrations on non-affiliates openly and without fear of repercussions. He didn't have a worry in the world, except for two worries: Erica and his seed. The last thing he learned from Jay was that he had a son and both the baby and Erica were fine. Erica was still in recovery and was expected to be amazingly back to normal. When Rick thought about it, he remembered back to when he prayed for all these outcomes. He smiled to himself. Shocka was watching TV from his cell door. He gave Rick his space to think, plus he himself didn't like to be bothered while his favorite talk show was on. Oprah, he loved him some Oprah. He even sometimes envied Stedman for wasting her life for so long and not marrying her yet. Rick made a fist and massaged his knuckles. They were a bit sore from him having to beat somebody up with them earlier in the day. He barely escaped the hole if it hadn't been for everybody minding their own business and not drawing a crowd. Rick's mind was flooded with thoughts of Erica and the baby. He was waiting for the pictures they took for him. They should be arriving soon, he thought. Rick got up and grabbed all his other pictures that Jay had sent him.

The sound of him opening the bag got Shocka's attention. He turned slightly from the door, saw there wasn't any food, then turned back to his show. Rick smiled and asked, "You hungry, Shock?"

"Whenever you wanna eat, I am," he replied.

"Gon head on and fix up sumpin', call me when it's ready."

Rick knew it was more than just family love why Shocka had Rick moved in the cell with him. Rick wasn't trippin, though. He knew he had so much money he could afford to buy the whole jail commissary. And sometimes it seemed like he did too. Sometimes, he even felt like they were using him or taking advantage of his kindness. He let the thought linger for a minute, then he shook it off because he knew how it is. A lot of guys really honestly need the help. Being in jail without no loved ones on the outside is a real sad case. People either forget about you or they just don't give a fuck about you. And nobody cares. It's like being alive dead. Rick felt it to be good that he could make somebody's life easy.

He sat back on his bunk and grabbed the first ten flicks. He kept his flicks organized with numbers on them and chronicled with the most precious ones being first. The first one was his mom. She stood next to Jason Sr. in her work outfit, smiling brightly. He favored this picture because this was the one he took of them the day Jason Sr. brought him and Jason Jr. a pair of matching Nike Cortezes. He smiled at that and flipped to the next shot. This one was of him and Jason at one of their parties dressed alike, holding two fine chicks on each arm. He remembered that day too. That was after their first official arrival at baller status. The rest of the flicks were of him and Erica in their condo. She would take pictures of him and he of her. She took one of him in his boxers laid out on the couch, sleep. He had slobber coming down the side of his mouth. She also took another one of him in the shower. It showed his bare ass soaped up. He smiled. He had one of his and her faces close up. His thumb was partially in the way from him snapping the picture. It was a couple of shots of her wedding ring and his too.

The next flick was what caused him to drop a tear. But you know how when you cry it's impossible to not get snot built up in your nose that causes you to sniffle. *Sniffle, sniffle, sniffle.* He did it. Shocka looked up from the spread he was making for them. First he didn't trip, but then, *sniffle, sniffle,* Rick did it again. That was Shocka's cue. "Look here, man, don't be in here cryin over no bitch, man, that shit'll get cha killed or tested."

At first Rick was about to flash on the old man for calling his woman a bitch, but he knew the old man was right. Even though this was a different and respectful cause for crying. But in jail, if it isn't a lost loved one or family member's death, you have to suck that shit up and man up. Rick lied. "Hell naw, I ain't cryin over no bitch, you got me fucked up in here! I got allergies." But the picture of Erica and her little bulge in her stomach brought those sniffles on.

Shocka turned back to cooking and truly not believing Rick's lie. But he didn't pry into it. He left well enough alone. The old man was tough, but he was smart too. Men will kill or be killed over their women. So the smart thing to do was just let Rick be.

Rick skipped past the other ones alike and went to the pictures of Jason's wedding. Seeing his boy all dressed up, and especially seeing KP dressed up, was what really made Rick laugh: thugged-out ass KP in a tuxedo. It looked like they all were having a ball too. Rick stared at Jason and couldn't help but wonder how much the tables had turned. Life can go from sugar to shit in a heartbeat. Jason just so happened to be living the lifestyle Rick was planning on living. Not that he was hating on his brother from another mother, but it was true. In fact, he was happy for Jason. His son, little Jason McMillian, wouldn't need for nothing. He or his mother. Rick still hadn't seen his son yet, though. He waited eagerly every day for those to come through the mail.

Shocka interrupted Rick's thoughts. "Food ready now," he stated solemnly. Rick packed all his flicks away and stood near Shocka. "Trip down memory lane, huh?" Shocka asked.

"Yeah, I miss all my folks, man. Plus my girl and my newborn. I already told you she just came up outta a coma, didn't I?"

"Yeah, you did, and that's a blessin, man. You owe the man upstairs a bundle."

Rick looked taken aback and asked, "I ain't know you was a religious dude, man." He smiled.

"I ain't, but I ain't stupid either. I ain't get to be this old by being stupid either. I know there's a God; shit, how else we all got here? Everything is a blessing, man, and that, your girl and yo baby, that was one big one love one. So preciate it."

"I will, I will and I do too."

Rick finished adding seasoning to his side of the meal because Shocka was on a low-salt diet. Afterward, Rick said grace and they ate. You'd be amazed at the meals inmates create in jail. And a spread, you could put just about anything in it. And that's what they did. Tuna, mayo, noodles, oysters, beef stick, cheese, rice, and some crackers on the side. Shocka hooked it up good. These white folks just don't know, most people rose up in the ghetto already used to eating that stuff, so it isn't anything new. And living in the projects is just like living on some penitentiary yard somewhere. So being in jail isn't anything new either. Same thing in jail, same thing on the street. Only thing missing is some real pussy. But a lot of fuck books, some Vaseline and lotion, and the work of your palm and five fingers, you aren't missing shit!

They finished eating and they lay on their bunks feeling stuffed like fat cats. Through the door, they heard a female's voice doing mail call. As she strolled by cells, you could hear dudes whistling and commenting on her sex appeal. Shocka jumped up, excited. He knew exactly who this was. She only filled in once before for the regular deputy. He waited and anticipated her arrival at his door. Rick wasn't excited at all for her. But he was anxious to know if he had some mail or not, though. He wasn't there the last time she had blessed the pod with her presence. Men hollered all types of obscenities to her. She was cool, though. She just smiled it off. She was used to this type of behavior from the men in jail. Even from her co-workers as well.

She finally made it to the door and stood there. Shocka was in view, lusting at her. She smiled. "Move, McCoy, you know you ain't got no mail."

"Yeah, I know," Shocka said playfully. "Don't nobody love me but you. When you goin' quit that job and come marry me, girl?" he smiled playfully.

"Move out my way, silly, I ain't tryin' to be in jail for givin' you no heart attack, boy, gon now." The whole pod laughed at her joke.

"McMillan!" she said, looking at Rick.

Rick jumped up, stated his jail number, and she handed him a stack of priority mail. Then she said, "Step to the window, McMillan."

Rick did so. He read her name tag as he did. "Yes, Ms. Baldwin?" he asked.

She gestured for him to put his ear to the crack of the door, then she said, "My man Tyrone told me to take care of you. He sends his love and he told me that you might need a relaxer. It's inside your mail. Let me know if you need anything. Anything except one thing. Cause that belong to one person." She smiled seductively and turned and sashayed provocatively away with an extra twist in her hip.

The men went crazy over her. She knew that Shocka probably overheard her but she also knew his C-file. He was definitely not a snitch. Plus the package had an extra little something in it for him especially.

Rick sat down quickly and tore through the mail. "Pictures" was scribbled on the front. There was a stack of them. The first one blew his mind back. It was his son. Their hair was the same exact color and his skin was the same pale color too.

"This my boy, this my boy, look at my boy, Shocka!" He handed the picture to Shocka reluctantly.

"Yeah, that's you there, ain't no denyin' that one, boy, that's you all the way."

Rick was already dropping tears at the sight of all the other ones. Shocka left it alone. He could understand those kind of tears. Rick just stared at all his pictures of Erica and his son. This was the best day Rick had in jail by far.

"You ain't gon open ya other mail?" Shocka asked.

Shocka knew it was some dope in it. He didn't care what it was; he just wanted to get high. So Rick opened it up, annoyed. Rick didn't get high. He already knew he'd most likely give all the crap to Shocka anyway. He opened up the package and there it was in plain view. Ms. Baldwin didn't have to hide shit. She was the police. She came straight through the front door with it. And there it lay. A lighter, some weed, some powder coke, and some tar of heroin. He handed the whole package to Shocka except the weed and the lighter. Shocka immediately tore through the tar, grabbed a spoon, put some water on it, and broke a small piece off the block and put it in the spoon of water. As soon as it diluted, he sniffed it up. *Sniff!* He repeated that about three or four times before he started to nod off into hop land. Ms. Baldwin forgot the zig-zags, so Shocka told Rick to tear a piece of that toilet tissue wrapper and use it. He did.

Rick said fuck it. He might as well go ahead and get high too just to relax and ease this pressure and stress he was in. After rolling one up, he did just that. For the first time in his life, he got high. And it felt good too. And he liked it. He grabbed his pictures, the ones of his son and Erica, and leaned back. He took two more puffs of the pinhead joint and gave it to Shocka. Rick was feeling better already. He smiled at his son in the picture and thought, "Life ain't so bad at all."

The End

ABOUT THE AUTHOR

I'm from East Oakland, raised in the heart of the ghetto, the Sixty-Ninth Village Project. I'm from an era where real ghetto life was and still is lived out in every element imagined in ghetto life. And all my stories have that real true ghetto reality expressed in them.